MURDE

C000051744

Also by Kulpreet Yadav:

MURDER IN PAHARGANJ

KULPREET YADAV

BLOOMSBURY
NEW DELHI • LONDON • OXFORD • NEW YORK • SYDNEY

© *Kulpreet Yadav, 2017*

First published, 2017

All rights reserved. No part of this publication may be reproduced or transmitted in any form or by any means, electronic or mechanical, including photocopying, recording, or any information storage or retrieval system, without prior permission in writing from the copyright holder.

No responsibility for loss caused to any individual or organization acting on or refraining from action as a result of the material in this publication can be accepted by Bloomsbury India or the author/editor.

BLOOMSBURY PUBLISHING INDIA PVT. LTD.
New Delhi London Oxford New York Sydney

ISBN: 978-93-86826-61-9

10 9 8 7 6 5 4 3 2 1

Published by Bloomsbury Publishing India Pvt. Ltd.
DDA Complex LSC, Building No. 4, 2nd Floor
Pocket 6 & 7, Sector C
Vasant Kunj, New Delhi 110070

Printed and bound in India by Thomson Press India Ltd.

The content of this book is the sole expression and opinion of its authors, and not of the publishers. The publishers in no manner is liable for any opinion or views expressed by the author. While best efforts have been made in preparing this book, the publishers makes no representations or warranties of any kind and assumes no liabilities of any kind with respect to the accuracy or completeness of the content and specifically disclaims any implied warranties of merchant ability or fitness of use of a particular purpose.

The publisher believes that the contents of this book do not violate any existing copyright/intellectual property of others in any manner whatsoever. However, in case any source has not been duly attributed, the publisher may be notified in writing for necessary action.

For my eldest daughter, Mehal Yadav, 'Jeanie,'
Your love, wit, and resilience have been a source of
abundant joy and inspiration for all of us.

ACKNOWLEDGEMENTS

I started to write this book almost three years ago, and I think it has been the toughest book for me to write. Always fascinated by the espionage theories and counter theories propagated by newspapers, I've curiously followed the games that people and organizations play with one another to serve the interests of their countries. Psychological warfare, counterintelligence or misinformation, bribing and cultivation of informants, deep-cover moles, sleeper cells, double agents, covert agents, honey-traps, etc., the daily fights happen right before our eyes, but we seldom take note. I've used my research and imagination to push the storyteller in me to whip up an engaging story.

I bounced this manuscript, in its different forms of readiness, off my close circle of friends and readers while I was writing it. In particular, I'm thankful to the following:

Shanti Perez for editing and helping me fine-tune the initial chapters.

My wife, Seema, and daughter Jeanie for their suggestions, which helped me cement the various events in the plot.

Sofia for reading through the entire book and suggesting changes towards the end.

Marian for a more detailed editing. This is the third book that Marian has edited for me, and I'm sure there will be many more.

Paul Vinay Kumar and Dipanjali Chadha from Bloomsbury India for believing in the story.

My agent and friend, Suhail Mathur, from The Book Bakers literary agency, who brought a rare energy and professional commitment to this work, for which I'm indeed thankful. I look forward to many more books with you, Suhail.

Jimmy of Jimmyeric Films & Media for an outstanding cover that I fell in love with as soon as I saw it and Sunny Lakharwal for the author picture.

I'm fortunate to have family and friends who believe in and support the storyteller in me. There would be little point in writing if I couldn't share the joy of publishing each new story with my friends and family who live in Delhi, Haryana, and elsewhere.

Mom and Dad, you are super awesome, super cool, and the best parents in the world. Thank you for your love and constant support.

Before thanking my readers, I would like to thank seven specific persons who not only stood by my side to support my Andy Karan series, published during the last two years, but also went out of their way to implement every conceivable marketing strategy to get my books closer to readers. Thank you, Anil Yadav, Praveen Kumar, Shankar, Sachin Yadav, Amit Yadav, Sanjay Singh, and Ajay Chourey.

And finally, many thanks to my small but growing audience of readers. Your support and encouragement are the reasons why I write. Do share your feedback after reading at kulpreetyadav@gmail.com – I'll be looking forward to your messages with great anticipation.

CHAPTER 1

Le Yogi Deluxe Hotel, New Delhi, Jan 28, 5 am.

THE DEAD WOMAN lay face-up on the bed, her hands at her sides. There was no blood, no bruises on the exposed parts of her body. Except for the eyes, which stared at the ceiling, one might think that in a moment, she would tilt her head and smile. Next to her on the queen-sized bed was a well-thumbed copy of the latest bestselling paperback. It was open and placed face down, as if she had put it aside briefly to talk to the killer.

A fake mink blanket was folded neatly on a chair beside the bed. There was too much order in the room for a crime scene. The room looked well lived in by a person who was neat and organized.

Vicks Menon bent forward into the dead woman's line of sight. Her eyes were a deep blue. There was no fear in them; there was no remorse. He wondered if the eyes knew that the body had died. How long could the eyes see after the heart stopped pumping? Was she watching him at this moment, her eyes sending signals to a still-not-dead brain that someone was staring at her? Her skin was very pale, and Vicks wanted to pull away, but something stopped him.

The woman was in a salwar kameez. This was a white woman—a dead foreigner wearing a blue silk salwar kameez, the tunic elaborately embroidered.

Vicks knew he was not doing the right thing. This was a police case, and he had no business being in the hotel room. He had arrived at seven this morning, and it was still dark when he stepped inside the seedy hotel in Paharganj, not far from the New Delhi railway station. Raju Arora, Vicks' friend, who worked as the night receptionist and doubled as the morning waiter to serve tea, had called him. Vicks had arrived fifteen minutes later.

'Did you inform anyone else?'

Raju was so gobsmacked that he couldn't utter a word for a few seconds. Then, slowly, he moved his head sideways. He was thirty, almost the same age as Vicks, but he had the innocence of a fifteen-year-old.

'Why did you call me?'

Raju hesitated before speaking, his eyes on the dead woman. Then, whispering as if she could still hear him, he said, 'You asked me to notify you if I noticed anything unusual in the Paharganj area.' He pointed a finger at the dead woman.

Vicks remembered now. Yes, he had asked his friends to inform him if they came across anything that was newsworthy. Anytime, 24/7. He wanted to do a few good stories, better than the ones produced by reporters working for the big magazines and newspapers. He had a point to prove: when it came to first-class journalism, he had a nose for the best stories, and when investigating a story, his instincts were the sharpest. Vicks had been out of work for the past two months but not out of ideas. And he had stopped drinking alcohol too.

A dead white woman in a cheap hotel was an unusually good story. No doubt about it. But he wanted to know more.

As a crime reporter, Vicks knew he couldn't risk leaving his fingerprints in the room. He had five years of experience to tell him that. But he also knew that human skin couldn't capture fingerprints, and by touching the body, he would be able to guess the approximate time of the victim's death.

Vicks extended his hand and very gently touched her cheek with his index finger. He paused before placing all his fingers and entire palm on her skin. He closed his eyes in concentration. Due to the process of *algor mortis*, which sets in right after death, her skin was cooler than the average human body temperature. Yet it was warmer than the room temperature, which he guessed was about twenty-five degrees Celsius. Vicks knew that the temperature of a human body dropped two degrees every hour after death. He made a mental note.

Vicks sidestepped the bed, walked to the other end of the room, and looked out the small window. Three floors below, in the foggy December morning, parked cars and tarpaulin-covered fruit and vegetable carts were silent as stones. There was no sound. Dogs, pigs, and people... the cold had silenced all life in Paharganj.

Just then, as if to prove otherwise, he heard the long, low whine of an approaching train.

Vicks turned and stepped closer to the bed. The new angle presented a different perspective. The neck was visible now, and he could see brown bruises. She'd been strangled. Probably by a person she knew well. Someone had walked in and said hello, she'd placed her book by her side, and then the killer strangled her.

Vicks looked closely and thought he could see a pattern in the bruises—centimeter-thick lines, three of them, with spaces in between. The killer's fingers.

He turned towards Raju. 'What's her name?'

'Sherry Bing.'

'Do you think anything was stolen?'

'Her suitcase is over there on the luggage rack.' Raju shifted uncertainly, as if he wanted to take two steps and open the closet to check.

'Don't.'

The shifting stopped.

'What did she use for identification when she checked in?'

'Copy of her passport.'

'American?'

'No, Israeli...' The rest of the sentence was a mumble. It was like he was thinking aloud.

Vicks looked at him and faked a smile, hoping to encourage him to divulge more. Minutes ticked by. In the end, Vicks asked, 'Where did she come here from?"

'She didn't note it in the register at the time of check-in, but...'

'But?' Vicks gave him a probing stare.

Raju Arora swallowed hard, dug his hand into the pocket of his dirty jeans, and pulled out a small, red slip of paper. 'The day she checked in, she dropped this. I thought I would return it to her later but never got the chance.'

Vicks snatched it out of his hands, gave him a smile, and peered at the paper. It was a bus ticket: Volvo, one person, from Udaipur to Delhi. The cost of the journey was 1000 rupees, and it was dated two days ago. It appeared that the woman had come to the hotel from Udaipur. When Vicks pursued the matter further, Raju said she'd arrived alone and remained indoors.

'Did she appear to be scared? Did she do anything you thought was abnormal?'

Raju moved his head sideways again, thinking.

In the lane below, a vehicle came to a screeching halt, disturbing the winter calm. Doors opened and closed. Dogs began to bark. Vicks looked out and saw two policemen in khaki enter the building, their sticks pointed at the mongrels to discipline them until they disappeared from view.

CHAPTER 2

'DID YOU CALL the police?' Vicks asked through clenched teeth.

Five foot nine and lanky, Vicks had piercing black eyes and a crew cut he'd been used to since childhood.

'No, no. Is it the police? Oh my God.'

Vicks left the room, Raju in tow. He whispered to his friend, 'Don't tell the police about me, okay?'

They waited near the stairs. When the footfalls floated up, Vicks pressed Raju's shoulders in reassurance and began climbing away from the sounds.

The roof was dark, just as he had expected. He crossed to the edge, jumped to the adjoining building, three feet away, and came down by the stairs. His golf cap was pulled down tightly over his head. There might be a camera in the lane, though the chances of its working were remote. Twenty minutes later, Vicks was home. He had taken a longer route than before. Just in case.

He pulled a bottle of Old Monk rum from the cupboard and looked at it greedily. He imagined opening the bottle and taking a gulp, the dark, heavy liquid clinging to his throat with a vengeance, like a long-lost friend, and burning all the way down. But he remembered his promise, and he put the bottle away.

Vicks had stayed away from alcohol for the past month. He was committed to following the advice of Tonya Mazumdar, his girlfriend. The two of them had been together until recently, when during an argument, she had walked out of his flat. And his life. Tonya's smell still hung in the bedroom, and Vicks missed her. But he had decided not to share his feelings with anyone, least of all Tonya.

Tonya was a clinical psychologist working part-time at the government-run All India Institute of Medical Sciences. They had met two years earlier, dated for a year, and moved in together six months ago. That was when the spark had begun to fade. There were issues, innocuous on the face of them, but annoying nonetheless. He had been adjusting as best as he could. Until the day he was cautioned by his boss at the *India Now* newspaper, where he covered the city crime and political beat. A month after the warning, the axe fell and he was handed his pink slip. He had done nothing wrong, had written all his stories as best he could. Vicks had no idea why his boss had called him casual and inefficient. He had even called him an alcoholic.

Tonya had claimed his drinking was the cause of their problems, but he knew better. Vicks had been fired from the newspaper for no mistake of his. That was the real problem.

Without a job, he had begun drinking more and more. The day of their fight, he had been drinking since morning and had said something nasty that he couldn't remember later.

At a mutual friend's party a week after Tonya left, he'd met her again. It was awkward, but when no one was looking, he'd whispered in her ear, 'Tonya, I have given up drinking.'

It probably sounded as if he was coaxing her to return, which he was. In response, she'd just left the party. The two of them had not met since.

The fact was that Vicks couldn't live without Tonya anymore. There were times he wanted her so badly that he almost dialed her number. But some of the irritation from that day's argument—the one he couldn't remember—had remained, and it kept his itching fingers in check.

Vicks remembered well Tonya's advice about his drinking problem. Yet this morning, all he could think about was having a drink. His soul needed the jolt that only alcohol could give as it crossed the blood-brain barrier. He kicked off his sneakers in frustration, both coming to rest upsidedown, and reclined on the sofa. The sofa had been Tonya's choice: blue with a velvet finish, varying shades of blue cushions on it.

But he wasn't thinking about her anymore. His eyes were closed to let the craving for alcohol pass.

After a few minutes, Vicks considered what he already knew.

A white woman, Sherry Bing, was found dead in a small hotel room in Paharganj, New Delhi. Probable cause of death was strangulation. There was no sign of a break-in, no sign of a struggle, and all her belongings seemed to be intact.

What was the killer's motivation?

It sure was a story. It was in Vicks' best interests to file the story as a freelance contributor to the *India Now* newspaper immediately. The new crime reporter would be sleeping at this hour, and Vicks could score some points with his old boss. Or maybe he could send it to a rival newspaper. He gave it some thought but in the end decided to remain loyal to his old employer.

Vicks typed the facts up on his laptop and copy-pasted the story into an email to his ex-boss after he was satisfied with the reread. He had also taken a picture of the scene of the crime with his cell phone. He attached that too. A picture, he knew as a journalist, was worth a thousand words. The article could be uploaded on the newspaper's website before their rivals even knew about the crime. He was about to click on 'send' when the phone's ringing interrupted his thoughts. It was Raju Arora.

He set his laptop aside, stretched his hands over his head, and stared at the Old Monk bottle with a brotherly affection before saying hello.

Raju's whisper was replete with fear and contained a stammer that he didn't usually have. 'Vicks, three more police jeeps have arrived... There are more than ten policemen asking me all sorts of questions... Whoever she was, she was someone very important.'

'Like hell. Since when did important people start staying at your hotel? It might be because she was a foreigner, and a white one at that.'

There was a pause, during which he felt his body tighten like a sprinter's seconds before the race.

'There are many men in plain clothes too. And a foreigner who doesn't look like a tourist. I think he is from one of the international embassies in the Chanakyapuri area.'

Something seemed to be brewing.

'I do not have a good feeling about this, Vicks.' Raju paused before adding, his voice difficult to discern now, 'I think I should tell them about you at this stage... Now. Otherwise, I might get into trouble if they find out later.'

Vicks understood Raju's dilemma. But if his name was given out, the police would start their signature harassment, which he knew so well from being a crime reporter. During big cases—and this one had all the right ingredients to become one—the police would pounce on the smallest of straws. Anything to take the public eye away from them and give them enough time to start their ruthless investigation.

Vicks had a name for such police actions, where all their time, focus, and resources converged to a single point. He called it *The Vortex*, a small space in which, if someone was unfortunate enough to be caught, he had to survive both the enemy and the police. And Vicks had no appetite for getting caught in *The Vortex*. Nobody had seen him come or go, and he had been careful not to leave fingerprints either.

'Nothing will happen. Just sit in a quiet room and tell yourself a hundred times that you didn't call me, and you'll be convinced of it. I never came to the hotel this morning, my friend, remember that.'

'I have to go now...'

The phone was disconnected. Vicks thought again about the bottle of Old Monk rum.

CHAPTER 3

IN THE CITY of Udaipur, 670 kilometers southwest of New Delhi, Jalaluddin was smiling. His brown eyes were fixed on the Monsoon Palace, the palace of the Mewar kingdom, which sat perched atop a nearby mountain. From where he sat in the courtyard of a heritage hotel, he could see the outline of the majestic old fort clearly.

To the hotel staff and his now-dead lover, Jalaluddin was Jamie, a Christian originally from Spain. His brown eyes, sharp nose, and athletic built were similar to those of people from the Andalusian mountains in the south of Spain. And he had learned his Spanish well, as a child in the London suburbs where he grew up. But in truth, Jamie was one of the three sons of a Shia Muslim couple from Iran who had immigrated to England a few years before he was born. His father was a tailor—a devout Muslim who offered namaz five times a day—and his mother a devoted housewife, content with the little that the family owned.

Jamie's thoughts were interrupted by the waiter, who placed a cup of coffee on the table next to him. He took a sip, and the simple luxury widened his smile. He felt safe.

A few days ago, he had been in a different heritage hotel with his girlfriend. The memory of her turned him temperamental. Being so much in her company for the last six months, he had started to like her. A momentary flash of anger erupted in his mind. She had been with him because that was exactly what was wanted of him. And now she was dead because that was exactly what was wanted of him.

He wiped away a drop of sweat that had slithered down his smooth forehead to rest on his right brow. It was not the coffee. It was the memory of the crime. Three days ago, Jamie had followed his girlfriend's Volvo bus from Udaipur to Delhi in a hired car with tinted windows. She was on her way to do some private errand, the details of which she refused to share with him. She'd even turned down his offer to accompany her to Delhi. When he said he would stay behind and wait for her, she had smiled.

Jamie had shared this development with his boss, and the excitement on the other end of the phone had been palpable. Now was their chance, he was told. She had gone to get something important, something that they desperately needed.

But once in Delhi, she didn't leave her hotel room for two days. Perhaps someone had visited during the night and escaped Jamie's observation. But he had been trained well and was, therefore, certain that he had not let his guard down for even a minute during the past forty-eight hours. He knew where her room was, and there was only one entrance to the hotel, which he had been watching while disguised as a vagrant. It had been easy to blend in with the locals. He only had to darken his face and hands ever so slightly and he looked like one of the millions walking the streets of New Delhi.

Most people begin to hallucinate due to lack of sleep after forty-eight hours. But not Jamie. He could keep his hallucinations at bay for sixty hours. Sadly, there was no backup in Paharganj, where he was working. When he couldn't keep his eyes open any longer, Jamie put on his gloves and slipped into the building. He had to find out what his girlfriend was up to.

Nobody saw him enter the small lobby, as the only receptionist was asleep. He stole the master key from his drawer, climbed the stairs to the third floor, and entered his girlfriend's room.

Surprisingly, she was awake. It was four in the morning. Was she expecting someone? She didn't hear Jamie as he pussyfooted closer, until he was just a step away. At that moment, his girlfriend looked up, smiled, and whispered, 'I knew you would come,' as if her wish had come true.

Jamie smiled too but stopped. He thought of telling her the truth. Thought of telling her that he was in her room not because he loved her but because he needed something she had. But he couldn't.

Whatever he was expected to find was here in this room. Probably. If he asked her, she wouldn't tell him and might even raise an alarm. That was something he couldn't afford to risk.

He bent down and gently brushed her lips with his, and then, as she put the book away, he squeezed her neck with all his might. She struggled but couldn't scream. He looked into her dying eyes, wondering what was she thinking, what her final feelings were. It was all over in a minute, slightly more. He removed his hands when her body slumped after a final, violent shudder.

Her struggle had left the sheets crumpled. Jamie lifted her and set her aside gently, as if he cared for her even now, and remade the bed. Then he placed her back on the bed, keeping the open novel, and even the page she was on, just as she'd left it.

Jamie was struck by an enormous desire to make love, like they had many times in the past six months, in Udaipur, Mumbai, and Goa. He smelt her hair, her face, felt the softness of her warm breasts, and whispered to his dead girlfriend, 'I liked you. I wish you were pure too, a Muslim like me. But you are not, and that's why you are my enemy. I hope you understand... understand that I had no choice.'

Jamie said this while looking into her eyes, which stared back at him. He sat in the chair and considered reading her paperback to let his thoughts wither away from the present, but couldn't. She had said she wanted to be a writer, a crime writer, and had, therefore, been reading more and more novels to master the art of writing. But instead, she had become a victim, a crime victim, of a man who was killing more and more to master the art of survival.

Jamie inspected her neck. There were no bruises. He searched her bag, her wallet, and all the nooks and crevices of the room during the next half hour, but didn't find anything unusual. What was she doing here, waiting all by herself? There was nothing on her: no suspicious devices, no documents, no pen drives, no CDs, no phone numbers, no scraps of paper with codes on them. Nothing. It was weird.

Jamie realized that he had been in her room for almost an hour and every second more was adding to the risk. Dawn was not far away. He slipped out of the room and peered out from behind the wall near the tiny lobby. The receptionist was still asleep and remained so as Jamie returned the key to its drawer and vanished into the cold night. He wanted to cry, but he knew he had sacrificed his feelings to the desires of God. It was going to be all right. God had always been on his side.

His boss grunted when Jamie informed him that there was nothing on her and hung up. When Jamie called him again after five minutes, he was given revised instructions. He hired a new taxi to return to Udaipur and came back to the hotel. Within minutes, he'd checked out. He'd wandered the city streets for a few hours with his small backpack and finally, when he got tired, checked into another hotel. His boss had told him to relax for a few days.

Jamie saw the lights on the Monsoon Palace turn on in the distance, 2000 feet above where he sat. Dusk had completely dissipated, and it was dark now. It was time for better indulgences. He laughed, awkwardly at first and then freely.

CHAPTER 4

VICKS PUNCHED THE air. He could feel the danger he was in. The uncertainty had created many unsafe scenarios in his imagination. But he wasn't going to take it lying down. This was his chance to prove that he was better than the other investigative journalists.

In a voice he was confident he controlled well, Vicks called his boss and asked him to check his email.

'I've already seen it, Vicks. Good work! The news is online now, and other media houses are copying it from us and crediting us. When will you give me more?'

The boss was ahead of him, the old son of a bitch. But Vicks had defeated the competition on this occasion. It was time to make his point.

'Where is that greenhorn now... the one you hired in my place?' He paused and, when his boss didn't answer, added more firmly, 'I want money.'

'In the next hour, fifty thousand rupees will be transferred to your bank account. Now, wherever you are, move your ass fast.'

'I want more money. I have to travel, eat, and maybe pay some bribes. Who knows what else? You know how it works.'

'The money is for you to get started, Vicks. You will get more as you go along. Now go.'

'Thank you, sir.' But his boss didn't hear him. He had already hung up.

Vicks got up and paced the drawing room of his small flat. He could feel the momentum of his thoughts increasing. Speaking to the boss had raised the bar. Now it was his story – Vicks' investigative story. He would prove what a big mistake his boss had made by firing him and might even be able to bargain for a better salary before he'd go back. Maybe try the newspaper's competitors too. To hell with loyalty. *India Now* was his boss's fourth newspaper in a career spanning ten years. Vicks had resisted all the temptations offered by others in the past, but after this case, he wanted to be a different man.

He rode his motorcycle to Paharganj and stopped in a lane that ran parallel to where the hotel stood. It was mid-morning, chaotic and raucous. It was easy to lose himself in the crowds of people coming and going. He parked his motorcycle, merged with the crowds, and began his approach. The hotel could only be reached from one side of the lane. On the other side, it ended in a cul-de-sac with a view of the park below. Years before, when Raju had first started working at the hotel, they had walked to this end sometimes to smoke their cigarettes.

It was for this reason that Vicks knew anyone with business at the hotel could approach it from only one direction. Even if his business was murder.

Without a doubt, the murderer had passed the same point on this lane at least twice: on his way to the hotel and, after the crime, on his way back. Which meant the chances of his being seen were doubled. A big plus. But the killer had come in the night. Vicks' confidence ebbed. He had pinned the time of the murder down to between four and five. The body had not yet begun to decompose when he had seen it, and the blood had not settled long enough to add a tinge of colour to the back and the parts of the body that rested on the bed.

At that hour, the chances of the killer being seen were remote. Almost nonexistent. People must have been asleep under layers of blankets, even the squatters on the roadside. But what if someone *had* been awake, unable to sleep? Someone sick? When sick, people's sleeping hours become random. It was a good starting point. Vicks clung to this possibility and decided to interview a few people in the vicinity. If he moved faster than the police, he could maintain the lead he already had.

Fifty meters from the hotel, Vicks stopped and tilted his head to let a car drive past. It was a black Ambassador. Someone important was being driven away from the scene of the crime. He looked at his watch. The top brass had arrived in less than three hours. That was fast. Any remaining doubt about the importance of the story evaporated.

From where he stood, he could see three vehicles, two jeeps and another black Ambassador, parked at the entrance of the hotel. More top brass. He noticed that there was a crowd of people around the area, which was probably cordoned off. He walked towards them and stood sandwiched between a ten-year-old boy and a betel-nut-chewing priest, who had a very big paunch ahead of him. There were murmurs all around him. He strained his ears to listen while he observed the hotel systematically from the outside.

There was a Delhi police constable at the entrance, staring at the crowd. He was frail, but with a Heckler & Koch MP5 rifle in his hand, he looked unflappable. A good weapon in any situation. But it was only for deterrence, Vicks knew, a purpose it was serving well.

An old, bald man came out. He was in plain clothes but was flanked by two uniformed police officers. He was whispering orders to them, which Vicks couldn't hear. He recognized the man in a few seconds: he was the Commissioner of Police for Delhi. A few steps behind the commissioner was a white man, about forty, eyeing the crowd suspiciously and looking every bit harried. Vicks made a mental note of him.

The police commissioner climbed into the car and was driven away. As the car passed the spot where Vicks stood, he noticed that the commissioner's forehead was furrowed in deep thought.

CHAPTER 5

As Vicks watched the policemen go back inside the hotel, he sensed the crowd's curiosity fade. The murmurs died down, and within seconds, the people around him began to wander away. Pretending to be someone who had only arrived a few minutes ago, he turned to the priest, who was still beside him, and asked him about the cause of the commotion.

'A *firangi* lady has died. They took the corpse away some time back.'

'Where did they take the dead body?'

'To the mortuary, where else?' The priest looked at Vicks, his eyes showing disgust at the stupid question.

'Of course.'

Vicks spotted a ramshackle tea cart not too far from where he stood. He walked over and asked for a cup before sitting on a bench adjacent to the cart. From this spot, he had a good view of the hotel. The tea seller was a talkative, middle-aged man who started telling the story of his life. This was good. Vicks encouraged him to continue talking as he surveyed the whole area. Where was Raju? He thought about calling him but decided against it. It wasn't safe to call.

Vicks waited there for almost two hours, during which he saw more policemen come and go. People from the media had also arrived, and a few who he knew waved at him from a distance. The most curious development was the arrival of a Toyota van containing four men in black sunglasses with Bluetooth headphones in their ears. Three entered the hotel on bouncy feet while one stayed outside, scanning the crowd. Vicks thought the man's head stopped for a moment when he looked in his direction. The man's shoulders were so straight that an army instructor would have been proud. All four men were white, just like the dead woman.

At the scene of the crime inside the hotel, Vicks imagined them disagreeing with the police over jurisdiction. Crimes involving foreign nationals always posed that difficulty. If the crime was committed on embassy soil, it was a different matter, and the laws of that country could be applied. But this murder was committed on Indian soil and had to be dealt with in accordance with Indian laws, as per statute. Yet there would still be some pulling and pushing, he was sure.

Vicks turned his attention to the Toyota. It had a CD number plate, which meant it was a Diplomatic Corps car. That was preceded by a numeric code, which Vicks noted in his cell phone so he could find out later which country's embassy the van was registered to.

At that moment, something that the tea seller was saying caught Vicks by surprise. He pulled his attention back to the man, who had mentioned one of his recent customers, drawing a comparison between Vicks and that man.

'Recently, there was someone like you, who just kept sitting here and drinking tea, staring at the hotel the whole time.'

'Can you tell me more about him?'

The tea seller looked around suspiciously and was suddenly at a loss for words. People who spoke too much sometimes ended up divulging information others wouldn't. It was a personality flaw Vicks knew well. The tea seller was now admonishing himself, his mumbling a garble.

'Tell me more about him,' Vicks repeated, this time slowly and deliberately, adding to the man's loss of confidence.

'Many people come here, sit the whole day... but it doesn't mean a thing. You have also been sitting here for a long time, does it mean anything?'

'Right.'

Vicks turned his attention back to the hotel. But his mind was on the tea seller. Half an hour later, when the tea seller signaled to a man who sat next to the cart with a mound of peanuts and left the place, Vicks got up too and followed him behind the shops. When they were out of sight of the hotel, he patted his back. The tea seller jerked in alarm and frowned when he recognized Vicks.

'You will tell me about that man now, or you will be in a lot of trouble.'

'Are you the police?' He seemed to be shaking with fear.

'I am worse.' Vicks stared into the man's eyes.

'Sir, a man had been hanging around in the lane for the last two days. He mostly sat by my cart, but his eyes were always focused on the hotel.'

'When did you see him last?'

'Yesterday night. When I packed up and left this place at nine, he was here. But I haven't seen him this morning.'

In the following ten minutes, Vicks found out what the man looked like and warned the tea seller not to share this information with anyone else, not even the police. He nodded and promised to call Vicks if he ever saw the man again.

CHAPTER 6

VICKS WAS IN Udaipur by nine that night. He had taken a Volvo immediately after getting the information from the tea seller. He'd thought of taking a flight but decided against it. His boss wouldn't give him more than the fifty thousand rupees he had already transferred into his account. Not unless the story kept hogging the limelight and Vicks got more and more material to keep his newspaper ahead in the race. When that happened, he had a bigger figure in mind. But first, he had to prove his worth.

In any case, a flight would only have saved him a few hours, due to the time it took for the check-in and check-out formalities at both airports.

Pulling his small bag over his shoulder, Vicks got off the bus, his eyes alert. There were people everywhere, as if an anthill had been kicked, a typical scene at any Indian bus stop.

He hired an auto-rickshaw and asked to be taken to the Fateh Sagar Lake. His further course of action would be planned at the lake. As the vehicle moved through the city, Vicks was taken back to his childhood. When he was about nine, he had come to live in Udaipur with his family. His father, an IAS officer, had been transferred from Nasik and had taken over as the Collector of the district.

Within days of their arrival, they had moved from a circuit house to a palatial house that he could recall even now. The house had had a big, circular driveway, a porch with white balustrade on the roof, and a colonnaded verandah around the main structure, which opened into a spacious living room from the front. During the time of the Raj, the house had been used by the British resident appointed by the Queen to the court of the King of Udaipur.

But the grandeur of the house soon became a curse for Vicks. His father, who habitually ill-treated his mother by shouting at her and insulting her in front of others, turned into a devil there. One night, when Vicks was quietly studying in his room, he heard a violent crash. His bedroom was on the second floor. He ran down the stairs into the living room and quickly reached his parent's bedroom, the source of the sound. He was just about to enter the room when he stopped instinctively. The door was ajar. His mother was sprawled on the bedroom floor, her eyes closed and blood trickling from the corner of her mouth. Vicks froze. He loved his mother; she was the greatest person in the world to him. When he emerged from his trance after a few seconds, he was too scared to turn his head. He had never experienced so much fear before. When he did, his eyes met those of his father, who stood breathing heavily, a golf club in his hand. Vicks slapped his hand over his mouth to smother a scream.

His father walked towards Vicks, the golf club slowly swinging in his hand. When he came to stop in front of him, Vicks dropped his eyes. A yellow pool had formed around his naked feet. He had peed his pajama. His father slapped him, and then it all went dark.

'We have arrived, sahib,' the driver said, bringing him back to the present.

Vicks paid him and looked at the vast blue lake, wiping sweat from his face. It was cold, but the painful memory made him feel hot from the inside. He removed his jacket and took a few minutes to mull over the reason he was in Udaipur. His blood screamed for alcohol, but as he thought of Tonya, part of his calm returned. He was going to win her back.

Vicks knew that he was not like his father. He respected women, and he was going to do everything right this time when he and Tonya got back together as a couple. The thought was enough to keep his worst nightmares in check for the moment.

On his way to the Delhi bus stand, Vicks had briefly stopped at RK Puram. One of his friends, who worked as a draftsman with the government, was waiting to rendezvous with him. This man had assisted Vicks in the past and was reliable. Vicks told him everything that the tea seller had said. Every single detail. The man heard him out thoughtfully, and after Vicks finished, he removed the pencil that was tucked behind his ear, pulled a piece of paper out of his hip pocket, unfolded it, and began to sketch. After five minutes, during which Vicks matched his quiet, the man extended his hand, the A4-size paper caught between his long fingers.

Vicks smiled and eased the paper out as if it were a thin gold sheet that demanded the utmost care. He then turned the paper over and brought it to the level of his eyes. He was now looking at the killer. Or someone close. It seemed like a reasonable starting point, and well worth the thousand rupees that Vicks paid the man for his services before he got back into the waiting taxi.

Now, with the paper carefully folded and stored in his bag, Vicks began to walk away from the lake.

His strategy was simple—start with the best hotels in Udaipur. Not that he thought the mystery man was there now, but if he had stayed earlier, people would recognize him. Perhaps. It was a long shot, but in this game of hide and seek, there were no shortcuts.

Vicks covered the top five hotels without any success. The security officers and receptionists had behaved just as he expected: important and aloof. All of them, without exception, gave him lectures on client confidentiality and reminded him of their loyalty oath. Vicks deflected their concern with smiles and bribes. His method didn't fail—it never had in the past either—but it set him back five thousand rupees.

Finally, at midnight, tired and disillusioned, Vicks checked into a seedy hotel and sent a text to Raju, hoping he would call. He wanted an update on what had happened after he left Delhi. The call came almost instantly.

'Vicks, there's big trouble. The Delhi police have taken over our hotel.'

'What do you mean taken over the hotel?'

Raju began to cry. Frustrated, Vicks repeated his question, trying his best to keep the irritation from seeping into his voice.

'All the people who were staying here have been forcibly checked out. Their money has been refunded, and now the entire hotel is filled with police. There are so many of them... They have dogs, funny equipment, and all kinds of guns. I'm very scared, Vicks. I am really very sorry.'

'This is not your fault, Raju.'

But Raju didn't stop crying.

'Okay, where are you?' Vicks thought that changing topic would help.

'I am in Shimla.'

'So it is all cool, since you're in a different city now. The police have taken over the hotel, not arrested you, and you have traveled two hundred kilometers away. So why are you crying?'

'I'm not worried about myself, Vicks.'

'Then—'

'I'm worried about *you*.'

Vicks was confused. 'Why are you worried about me?'

'I told them about you, Vicks. I'm very sorry.'

'You what! You idiot, why did you tell them my name?'

'I had to, Vicks. They said if I didn't... they would torture me.'

The line went dead.

CHAPTER 7

VICKS TRIED TO call him back, but without success. He gave up after a few more attempts. The philosophy that it was better to have a wise enemy than a foolish friend struck him with its perfect relevance. His first thought, when he finished considering the repercussions, was of drinking rum. He wanted to calm his nerves. The news had stunned him, and he had no doubt that the Delhi police now considered him their prime suspect, a scapegoat they would happily go through hell and high water to find. *The Vortex* was staring him in the face.

The first thing he had to do was get rid of his phone. He didn't want to receive any calls from the Delhi police. Vicks swiped his smartphone open and immediately put it in non-transmitting mode. It meant that he could use the camera and all the other applications, but not call or receive calls. He breathed easier, knowing that the police could not call him now, relieved that they hadn't called him earlier. But now the challenge was how to remain in touch with Tonya and his boss. What if they had something for him and wanted to call him? Vicks needed a local phone. He knew he could buy one off the shelf with cash, but not in the dead of night.

Vicks considered the two choices he now had: either turn himself in or become a fugitive. Both were suicidal.

His thoughts turned towards Tonya, his relief valve. He needed to speak to her badly, hear her voice, and tell her that even while in such big trouble, he had stayed away from alcohol. That he had kept his promise.

It took him two hours to think straight. He finally decided to keep under cover for as long as he could. In any case, he was safe until the police found him. Unless Raju told them about the bus ticket to Udaipur, and they came looking for him. Vicks gave himself a window of one day.

At dawn, Vicks called Raju from the phone in his hotel. It was a risk, but he had to know something else. He had to be sure.

'Sorry Vicks,' Raju said. 'There was no signal after our call got interrupted last night. Are you okay, and why are you not calling me from your cell phone?'

Vicks nerved himself up to say, politely, 'I hope you have not told the police about the bus ticket to Udaipur.'

'Hell, no. How could I do that? I can't throw you to the dogs; I'm your friend, Vicks.'

Vicks couldn't suppress his laughter. After letting him down, Raju was innocently pleading not guilty. It lightened his mood a wee bit, and he thanked Raju before hanging up.

When Vicks called Tonya, once again using the hotel phone, it was six in the morning. The phone rang for a long time before it was answered, and her voice had the heaviness of someone just awakened. To stem the awkwardness of two people in a strained relationship, Vicks decided to keep his call businesslike. Before calling, he had practiced his side of the conversation a few times. He was calling her for help, and that was exactly how he wanted to start out.

'Tonya, I am sorry to wake you so early, but I need your help.'

'Tell me.' It was a relief that she kept her side of the conversation businesslike as well.

'I'm investigating a story... about that dead foreigner; you must have seen it in the news.' He paused, then continued when Tonya didn't interrupt. 'I was the first one to reach the crime scene. Courtesy Raju Arora. I sent the story with a picture to *India Now*, and they've uploaded it to their website. Everyone else took it from there.'

'Hmmm.'

Vicks continued, 'I know where the killer came from and roughly what he looks like.'

'What do you want from me?' Her businesslike approach was becoming less of a relief and more difficult to put up with.

Vicks swallowed and said, 'I want you to help me profile this killer. I will email you all the details. It will help me find him, and if I do, my boss might take me back at a better salary and kick the present investigative reporter out. I will be at this number for a couple of hours more. There's a problem with my phone, but I'll have a new number later in the day and will pass it on to you.'

'Okay, send me the details, and I'll see what I can do.'

Vicks breathed easier. Now was the time to add a bit of a personal touch. 'I haven't consumed a drop of rum since you left. Thought you should know.'

'Thanks.' And she hung up.

Thanks, thought Vicks, surprised.

He quickly opened a word document on his laptop and typed up all that he knew about the crime, along with the details the tea cart seller had told him. Satisfied that he had not forgotten anything, he emailed the document to Tonya.

CHAPTER 8

TONYA READ THE email while still in bed, leaning against some pillows propped against the headboard. A thick quilt covered her body, but she wasn't feeling cold anymore, thanks to Vicks' phone call, followed by his email.

Tonya was five foot four and had big eyes and a cheerful, round face, which was sorrowful at the moment. Her shoulder-length hair was down, and her curls bounced as she walked across to the kitchen. Tonya knew she was beautiful, but when Vicks appreciated her looks, she felt wanted. The memory of the day she walked out of his house still lingered in her mind. But he had left her with no choice.

She was still in love with Vicks. Of this, she had no doubt whatsoever. She had been angry with him for his drinking problem, but she believed that with love and care, the problem could be resolved.

When they were together, she had spoken with Vicks at length about his past and had an idea what caused him to binge-drink.

She regretted having to take the extreme step of moving out of his house, but that day, consumed by anger, she had lost control of herself. Momentarily. He had been drinking since morning, blaming his boss and the others at the office for the loss of his job. When

Tonya reasoned that he should try to look inward instead, he had gotten angry and started to verbally abuse her. The look in his eyes, the hate they spewed, had snapped something in her head.

Tonya had quickly packed her suitcase and bolted out, while Vicks kept sitting in the living room, drinking more and more. When she opened the door and turned to look at him one last time, he didn't even lift his head. She slammed the door and walked out.

But now Vicks had asked her for help.

She knew that if she stayed away from him any longer, Vicks would fall prey to alcoholism again. His call gave her a good reason to patch things up. She was happy that he had been keeping his promise.

She reread the email. The details Vicks gave were straightforward and helped her picture the crime scene clearly.

Tonya was a psychologist and had interned at the All India Institute of Medical Sciences after completing her doctorate at Jadavpur University in Kolkata. Now she worked part-time at AIIMS, and one of her jobs was to do criminal profiling for the Delhi police. Criminal profiling, an abstract science that relied upon intuition and used data about the crime scene to offer insight into the criminal and his motive, was her forte, and everyone regarded her as one of the best.

In the past two years, her profiling had helped the Delhi police narrow down the suspects in a number of cases. On one occasion, it had resulted in the capture of a criminal who was nabbed by the police just as he was about to kill another unsuspecting victim. She had met the Delhi Police Commissioner a number of times and knew many Assistant Commissioner of Police officers.

Once again, Tonya reread the information that Vicks had sent. Then again and again, until she was confident that she had internalized all the details.

She picked up her cat, Mishty, responded to her shrill *meow* with a *good morning*, and began to brew coffee. Outside, it was still dark. Five minutes later, she was seated at the dining table, her laptop open in front of her and Mishty licking the soles of her feet. The strong cup of coffee had helped kickstart her brain, and ideas were beginning to form. She typed them out, describing the scene of the crime from the viewpoint of the killer, her favourite method.

> CRIME: *The victim was killed by someone who cared for her. He took pains to restore the condition of the bed. A quick death was intended, as there were no other injuries. The killer struck after waiting for two days. He searched the room thoroughly.*

> WHEREABOUTS: *The victim came from Udaipur, and it was likely that she was in a romantic relationship with the killer.*

> THE KILLER: *A ruthless male who worked for someone else. But he seemed to have a soft spot for the victim. Young, about thirty, organized, and focused.*

> MOTIVE: *The victim had something that the killer wanted.*

Tonya walked around absentmindedly, thinking about what she had written. Her job was to create bridges between what was real and what was logical to make investigations easier.

Two more coffees later, she emailed her report to Vicks, promising to refine it over time and asking him to share everything he could. *Please be careful*, she added at the end. She wanted to sign off with *I love you* to ease her lover's nerves, but something stopped her. Perhaps she needed to give it more time. Only when lovers are separated do they realize how much they are in love. Separation is the real litmus test.

She ended her message with her name, looked down, and whispered to Mishty, 'I love you, Vicks.'

CHAPTER 9

ARIEL MILLER STOOD in front of the hotel in Paharganj, his arms folded across his chest. He was surprised by the number of police vehicles parked in the vicinity. Earlier, he had tried to enter the hotel's front gates but was asked to back off by cops holding automatic rifles. Something was amiss.

Ariel was sure that he was in the right place. Sherry Bing was supposed to meet him at this very hotel. She had confirmed that she would wait for him. Was she still inside? Though he had read an article about a dead foreigner in the morning newspaper, the press had not disclosed the names of the hotel or victim.

He had a sinking feeling, as he was three days late. But his experience had taught him not to jump to conclusions in such situations. In his world, putting two and two together more often than not resulted in five, not four. He turned the collar of his jacket up to protect himself from a sudden gust of cold wind and looked up. Vultures were circling in the sky. This was a game of patience, and he decided to wait and watch.

Ariel was a slight man, five foot seven, with a face dotted with pimples. His eyes were small and deep-set, and his nose was abnormally long and crooked. When he was still in school, his friends had mocked him, calling him Mr. Ugly. But Ariel was sharp and had confronted them with his higher scores on the day grades were announced. As he grew older, he turned into a loner and continued to do well in his studies. After completing college, he shunned the jobs that came his way and chose to travel instead. He despised sharing his workspace with other people. His fear of being ridiculed about his looks ensured that he stayed out of regular jobs.

When he turned twenty-five, his father, who was a local merchant in Tel Aviv, summoned him after one of his trips and told him to get a job. It was a warning, his father said; if he couldn't find a job in a month, he would have to move out of the house. Ariel was devastated. If there was one person in the world who had never said anything bad to him, it was his father. He left his home that very night. After a week, when he had run through what little money he had and begun to starve, a man approached him.

Ariel was seated in the shade of a tree across from a café in the busy Carmel market in his hometown. He had not eaten for two days and was desperate.

'First, let's go and eat,' was all the man said.

Ariel saw no harm in accompanying the stranger to the café for food. After they had eaten, he shared the story of his life with the man. He didn't hold anything back. The man nodded and held out a copy of Ariel's college transcript. As Ariel looked at him, confused, the stranger offered him a job.

'This job,' he said, 'doesn't require you to be in the company of anyone. You will work independently, get the chance to travel a lot, and earn a salary plus expenses.'

Ariel grabbed the opportunity with both hands and was sent for training the very next day.

After training rigorously for three years, Ariel, now an Israeli intelligence operative, went to Tehran on his first assignment. He stayed undercover there for over five years, reporting his findings through established secret channels using a mixture of people and technology. Recently, however, the enemy had finally got wind of his existence. But before he could return to Tel Aviv for his next assignment, he had one job to do—deliver a message to Sherry Bing from her father.

Sherry's father was also an Israeli spy based in Tehran. Ariel had learned that the other man had been compromised and was being held as a spy by Iranian intelligence. Before a similar fate befell Ariel, he escaped Iran and reached Delhi via Pakistan, still carrying the letter Sherry's father had managed to hand over to him. Once he arrived in the capital city of India, the first thing he did was contact the Israeli embassy from a phone booth outside the airport.

When he reached the embassy, Adam Shatner, the defence attaché at the embassy, replied to his greeting and said, 'Shalom! So who are you and exactly what business are you on here in India?'

That was the trouble. Ariel had been under deep cover for so long that he was not sure how to tell Adam who he really was. So he didn't. 'I'm a tourist on a visit to India.'

The defence attaché excused himself, and while Ariel waited in the interview room, found out that Ariel was lying.

Adam Shatner's overreaction was something that Ariel hadn't anticipated. His troubles were instantly compounded, as he was asked more and more uncomfortable questions. He couldn't tell Adam that he had traveled for several days on foot, hitchhiking through the rugged north of Pakistan, and finally caught a bus from Amritsar on documents forged for him by a man in Lahore. After arriving in Delhi, he went to the airport only so he could use an airport taxi for his trip to the embassy. Ariel had never imagined his arrival would be taken so seriously and his cover blown.

Perhaps five years out of the loop had left him out of touch.

Ariel was arrested even as he demanded a meeting with the ambassador. Finally, he was taken blindfolded to a safe house. While in detention for the next three days, he cursed himself for not meeting Sherry Bing first to deliver the message. Then, on the fourth day, as suddenly as he'd been arrested, he was let off.

This time, he didn't make any mistakes. It was time to use the only number he'd been given for life- or- death emergencies. Once he was a few kilometers from the embassy, he called his contact in Tel Aviv from a phone booth. The voice on the other end of the phone asked him to wait for a day so the ambassador could be informed about his status through proper government protocols. Ariel was alive, and therefore, time was not a problem.

He'd had no idea that the detention by his own countrymen would cost him so dearly. When he finally found out that Sherry Bing was dead, he sat down on the edge of the road near the hotel in Paharganj, suddenly dizzy.

He had failed. Ariel Miller, top of the Mossad class of 2002, had failed. He had failed to deliver the final message of a father to his daughter.

CHAPTER 10

VICKS READ THE profile of the killer that Tonya had sent. It added to his confidence and confirmed some of his own assumptions. Though there was nothing substantial in her profiling, he liked the part where she said that the killer had probably been in a relationship with the victim. That meant that the killer and Sherry Bing might have been together. And since she had arrived from Udaipur, they must have stayed in the city together. If he showed both their pictures to hotel staff, instead of one, the chances of recognition were higher. The killer could still be in Udaipur, though the chances of that were remote.

Vicks pulled out his smartphone and looked at the pictures of Sherry Bing. He had taken two pictures at the scene of the crime. One from the top, the victim's face and part of her torso filling the frame, and the second from the side, with her full body visible. It was the second picture that he had sent to his old boss at *India Now*, since the face was not recognizable. The second picture camouflaged the victim's identity well and could, therefore, be freely used in media reports.

Vicks had not shared the first picture with anyone. Not even with Tonya when he sent her the details that morning. While investigating in the hotels the previous evening, he had also not used her picture. His interest was in the killer, not the victim. Showing a picture of a dead foreigner to hotel security staff was stepping far too deep into police business.

Vicks stepped out of his small room, walked down a dark corridor, climbed down a narrow flight of stairs, and arrived in the lobby of the hotel he had been staying at. Four cane chairs were arranged around a red plastic table opposite the small reception desk. Three were occupied by men in colourful headgear, who looked blankly outside at the street as they sipped tea in conical clay cups. He sat down in the single empty chair. A boy of about fifteen was behind the wooden counter. In comparison to the picture of Salman Khan that hung behind him on the yellowed wall, his face seemed narrow and malnourished. Vicks smiled at the boy, who yawned in response, his eyes heavy, like those of a night watchman. He looked like someone from a village who had spent the night under a bridge in the big city.

Vicks picked up the newspaper that was lying on the plastic table. It was a local Hindi daily. The main story was about the murder of a foreigner in Paharganj, Delhi. The police, it added, had several confirmed leads as the investigation rolled into the second day. Printed next to the story was a picture of Sherry Bing, photo courtesy of the *India Now* newspaper. It was the same picture he had sent to his editor.

Vicks wondered what those leads could be. He thought about Raju but breathed easy, as Raju had said that he had not mentioned Udaipur to the police.

He pulled a second newspaper out from under several others. This one was in English, and the Delhi police's disclosure about having a lead was a boxed story on the side of the page. More details were included in it. By the time Vicks finished reading, he was sweating. The police had said that the killer came from the state of Rajasthan. They didn't mention Udaipur, but Vicks thought they were holding back some information.

Who could have told them about Rajasthan? Since there were no witnesses to do so, Vicks was no longer sure whether Raju had been speaking the truth.

It was time to take the bull by the horns. He looked at Sherry Bing's picture on his phone once again and decided to put the phone in transmitting mode for a couple of hours in case Tonya or Raju called to update. Soon, he would acquire a new number.

An hour later, Vicks checked out of the hotel and resumed his inquiries at local hotels using both photos: the sketch on paper and the picture on his smartphone. He was now concentrating on the hotels preferred by western tourists, based on their reviews on the TripAdvisor website. An hour later, he struck gold when one of the receptionists stared at the two pictures and said, 'This couple has visited our restaurant many times.'

Vicks pressed him for more, barely containing his excitement.

'But,' the man said, 'I'm sure that they were not staying in our hotel. They used to come only in the evenings for dinner.'

'Do you know which hotel they were staying in? Do you know their names?'

He shook his head.

Vicks was dejected. But there had to be a way to capitalize on this piece of information. 'Perhaps we could check their credit card payments.'

'But... I have no idea which days they came. And also, I have no idea whether they paid in cash or on a card.'

'Can you give me access to the CCTV footage?'

The receptionist, a local young man with spiky hair and bright eyes, suddenly lost steam. 'I am sorry; I can't allow that. Only the security manager is authorized.'

'Tell me where I can find him, and I will talk to him now.'

Someone tapped Vicks on the back. He turned in alarm and came face to face with a dark- complexioned man with bloodshot eyes.

'Please step this way,' the man hissed, his voice more a warning than a request. Before Vicks could respond, he felt the man's rough hands physically pulling him away from the reception desk. He cooperated and headed in the direction the man wanted him to take. He was walked into a room, pushed hard, and the door slammed. Vicks lost his balance and nearly fell but luckily managed to save himself from the fall.

'What the fuck?' He turned, angry.

'I have been hearing a lot about you since yesterday, mister. If you want to stay out of trouble, tell me who you are.'

Vicks thought about the hotel staff he had met yesterday. They must have been talking with each other about this weird man going around, showing a photograph and asking for private details in exchange for money. Not a legal thing to do. Which meant he was in a very weak position, on shaky moral ground, for reasoning with the beast in front of him. The situation required tactful handling.

'Who are you? Out with it now, or I will call the police,' he barked, his eyes redder as he began breathing more heavily, like an animal preparing to go in for the kill.

Vicks knew he had very little time to react. But he couldn't tell the man the truth. 'Sir, the man in the picture has borrowed money from me—a hundred thousand rupees—and he is not responding to my phone calls. The address he gave me is fake, so I'm searching for him. He likes the good life, and I thought he might be staying in one of the luxury hotels.'

The man with the red eyes relaxed a little, and Vicks knew he'd been successful in misleading him. 'Why don't you go to the police? Why are you wasting your money bribing hotel staff?'

'You know how the police are... they will ask for their cut, which would be much higher than what I will spend if I do it myself.'

'Shut up,' the man barked.

He pulled out his mobile phone and spoke to someone in a low voice, which Vicks couldn't make out. After disconnecting, the man took a step closer and pulled a pistol out of his jacket. He raised the pistol to Vicks' head and smiled wickedly. It was the smile of a killer, the smile every victim sees only seconds before his death.

CHAPTER 11

ARIEL TOOK AN auto-rickshaw back to the embassy. He had no place else to go. It had taken him ten minutes to come to terms with the situation at Paharganj. He was not sad about Sherry Bing's death. He believed in the simplest of life's philosophies: that everyone had to die one day. His suffering came from somewhere else—the fact that he had failed to deliver a father's message to his daughter.

He sat on the grass across the road from the Israeli embassy, stared at the camera mounted on the wall, and hoped like hell that his identity would be restored fast. He had no money, a fake passport, and no change of clothes. He needed a bath, some cash, and a comfortable place to rest before he could think further.

His thoughts turned to Sherry's father. Late at night a few weeks back, he had woken to the sound of light tapping on the door of his home in Tehran. He'd eased it open with one hand, a cocked pistol behind his back in the other. The rusty hinges on the door whined noisily, drowning out his racing heartbeat. Had his identity been compromised?

There was the shadow of a solitary man at the door. The man stood awkwardly, as if he was injured. Ariel looked beyond him. There was no one.

He heard the man whisper in Hebrew, 'I need help.'

Ariel asked the man to step in, asking simultaneously in Persian, 'What did you say?'

The man entered the house and took the chair in the small living room that Ariel pointed to. Then he smiled and whispered the code words. The code Ariel had not used once in the last five years. The code that could only be used in person, never on the phone or internet. The code that differentiated a friend from an enemy.

The man waited patiently as Ariel put his pistol away and replied with the proper code words. With identification established, the two men hugged each other.

The man told Ariel that the Iranian intelligence service was watching him and he should leave the country as soon as possible. 'Go without leaving a trail, and fast,' the old man said.

Ariel nodded. The man had a lot of wounds on his body. 'How did you get those?'

'I was tortured.'

Ariel got to his feet. How could they? Anger flooded his mind. 'Tell me more. I will avenge the pain inflicted on you.'

The man smiled. 'No need, please.' He gave Ariel a folded piece of paper and continued, 'Please take this to my daughter. She is in India, and her name is Sherry Bing. Give this to her and tell her that I am well. Also, tell her that perhaps I will never come back. And that I love her.'

'What's in the letter?'

'It's a code I taught her as a child. No one else knows it. She will understand what to do. Promise me that you will give it to her.'

'I promise.'

The old man said that the Iranian intelligence service had proof that he was an Israeli Jew. They were not sure whether he was a spy, but they were torturing him to find out more. 'Perhaps they will kill me,' he said.

'I am sorry.' Ariel didn't know what to say as he took the letter and pocketed it. The old man left soon after. Ariel checked the time. It was three am, and no one seemed to be lurking outside the house.

He couldn't sleep and, at six that morning, made himself a cup of the rose-petal-infused Iranian tea that he was used to. He turned the radio on and heard a special announcement: a statement by the government that they had executed an Israeli spy that morning. The announcement made Ariel nervous. He turned the television on, and his worst fears were realized as he saw a picture of the old man from the previous night, a gunshot wound in his head.

Yet Ariel was relieved. The old man was lucky that he had not been tied to a pillar and stoned to death. Perhaps they were not entirely sure that he was a spy and had killed him to be on the safe side.

He decided to leave the house quickly. What if the old man was followed? Carrying a suitcase or bag with him would attract attention, so Ariel just walked out casually, hands in the pockets of the jacket he was wearing. He had sufficient Iranian rial and Pakistani rupees to last for a few days.

And now here he was in New Delhi, an identity-less man who had failed the simple errand of passing on a letter. He took out the piece of paper out of his pocket and peered at the jumble of English letters. There were words, sentences, and paragraphs, but it made no sense. The old man had mentioned a secret code, but now, with both the daughter and father dead, perhaps the message would never be read. He pocketed it and looked up at the clouds. The openness relaxed him, and he eased back to lie on the grass.

Sherry Bing had been on a vacation in India. Ariel had called her from Lahore as he waited in a hotel while the last of his money was being put to good use to make his fake identification papers. He used the number her father had given him to fix a rendezvous, hoping to meet with her soon. She was on a vacation with a friend, she said, and could reach Delhi the next day. He particularly remembered her voice, which was soft and mellifluous, like that of someone who had learned recently how to sing.

Using the internet, he found a cheap hotel in the backpacker's den of New Delhi called Paharganj and gave her the name of it. But he had no idea how much time would it take for him to reach Delhi. She said she would wait for him. It was simple. And now she was dead.

Who could have killed her? Was her death in any way connected to his conversation with her father? The stickiness of the question made Ariel feel that he was only far from Iran, not from danger.

When he sat up, he was face to face with someone he had begun to hate.

'We need to talk,' said Adam Shatner, the defense attaché of the Israeli embassy, a wry smile on his lips.

Chapter 12

VICKS STARED AT the pistol. He wasn't prepared to believe that the security manager of a five-star hotel would kill him in cold blood in a room right next to the reception desk. It wasn't possible. There were too many people in the lobby outside. He could hear the chatter of people at the reception desk, checking in or checking out. The sound of a gunshot could not be contained by these walls. In any case, he had done nothing so grievously wrong as to be killed.

His thoughts kept him cool. The man with the red eyes shoved his free hand into his pocket and removed a short barrel. When he began screwing it onto the pistol, Vicks realized what it meant. A *silencer*.

Vicks began to sweat, frightened of the man who was screwing the menacing extra barrel on the pistol, staring into his eyes the whole time. With the silencer on, perhaps no one outside would ever know a bullet had been fired. Sweat ballooned in Vicks' armpits and began to trickle down his back. He felt the grave fear of death staring at him.

Finally, after what seemed like an eternity, the man asked him again, his voice a whisper this time, 'Who are you?'

'I am a journalist.'

'What do you want?'

'I am looking for a story.'

The door opened, and an old man walked in from the lobby, accompanied by a female member of staff. The man was out of breath, and the woman seemed worried. The man with the red eyes shoved the pistol and silencer into his pocket and turned.

'Sir, please help. This gentleman is not feeling well,' she said, harried, to the red-eyed security manager.

This was his chance, thought Vicks. He walked straight out of the room, and once he was in the lobby, he ran through the front doors out to the porch and onto the road seconds later. He kept on running, taking random turns, scared to even look back, until he was tired and out of breath. When he finally did turn back, there was no one behind him.

He was standing next to a café. He ducked inside and asked for water. His phone began to buzz as his nerves were calming down and his brain had begun processing the information. He took out his phone. It was his boss.

'Hello.'

'Vicks, where have you been? Where is the next part of the story, Mr. Reporter?'

'I am working on it, sir.'

Vicks heard nothing for a few seconds except his boss's heavy breathing. 'Okay, let me share with you the dream I had last night. I saw you, Vicks Menon, drinking in a bar and getting drunk with my money.' He paused, and when he resumed, he was shouting. 'Drinking with my bloody money.'

'Fuck you, you sonofabitch,' shouted Vicks. But his boss had already hung up. Like always, his boss had had the last word. He thought of calling him back and abusing him, but drank some more water instead and took five long breaths. It was something that Tonya had taught him to do. Within minutes, he saw that calling back would have been the wrong thing to do. He silently thanked Tonya.

There was a mirror on one of the walls of the café. Vicks stared at his reflection, relieved to be alive. He tried to smile, but the muscles of his face refused to obey his brain.

Had the man really intended to kill him? Why? Why was the man disturbed about his asking questions about the suspect? Did he know him? Was he harbouring him?

Vicks removed his shoulder bag and took out his laptop. In a few minutes, he was checking the names of the staff on the hotel's website. In no time, he saw the red-eyed man staring into the camera. The picture was old, but it was definitely him. His name was written next to the picture: Amar Rathore, Security Manager. His email address and cell phone number were also listed. Vicks noted it all down and began to browse the other pages.

The hotel was called the Welcome House Resort. It was a standalone heritage property with no affiliation to any of the well-established chains. He read the information about the hotel and realized that it had once been a palace belonging to one of the royal families of Udaipur. The palace was refurbished in 1969 and turned into a luxury hotel. It was on the banks of a beautiful lake and was one of the most popular hotels with the rich and famous from Bollywood and Hollywood.

There were many pictures. He browsed through them. There was Akshay Kumar and Twinkle, Kareena and Saif Ali Khan, Shahrukh with someone he didn't recognise, Brad Pitt and Angelina Jolie, and... His fingers stopped at a couple next to Julia Roberts. He enlarged the screen and shifted the focus to the couple. There was no doubt. It was Sherry Bing, holding hands with her lover. He was surprised by how much the sketch matched the person staring at him from the laptop screen.

More questions began to form in his mind. If Sherry Bing had visited this hotel with the man who Vicks now knew was her killer, why did she choose to stay at such a cheap hotel in Delhi? And why had she been alone, rather than with her lover? What was she hiding from him? And why did the man disguise himself and keep watch outside the hotel? What did he suspect the woman of doing?

He was confused and tired. But alive. The final thought kicked in some adrenalin, and as Tonya's face flashed through his mind, he was back in business. He called her using the café's STD and filled her in about all the latest details but didn't tell her about the attack. Then he asked her to check the picture on the hotel's website.

'Which picture, Vicks? There is no picture of Julia Roberts,' her concerned voice floated back after a minute.

'But I can see it on my laptop.' Vicks refreshed the webpage and was taken aback. The picture was no longer there. He quickly navigated to the staff page and saw what he'd suspected. The name and picture of Amar Rathore had been removed too. That meant someone was working away at the website at that very moment.

'What happened, Vicks?' Tonya's concerned voice reached him as if from the bottom of a well, as the initial shock wave washed over him.

'The picture has been removed, Tonya. And so have the details about Amar Rathore, the security manager who tried to kill me.'

'Kill you?'

Vicks regretted mentioning it. He explained everything that had happened at the hotel and promised to take care before hanging up.

CHAPTER 13

Tonya was furious. Someone had tried to kill Vicks when all he wanted to do was get a story. The details mentioned by Vicks were moving in her mind like a gathering storm.

She knew she was in love with Vicks. Although she had left him, the feeling had not died. The news of the attempt on his life shocked her. She had not realized the intensity of her love for him...until now. What if the attacker had succeeded? The thought sent shivers down her spine. No, she would not let anything happen to Vicks. He had to be saved. The time had come to not only revise the profile of the killer but also seek the help of the police to ensure that Vicks was safe.

The killer was better networked than she'd thought. No doubt about it. He had people working for him too. His real intentions were deeply hidden, and probably he was well-funded, if his lifestyle was anything to go by. He had killed the victim ruthlessly to acquire something that she had. How many pleasurable moments must he have spent with her, if he was indeed her lover? And yet he didn't hesitate to kill her.

Tonya paced her office in the hospital. She paused and looked out the window. Two floors below, she could see people sitting in the sun in the small park. A couple caught her eye. They were sharing food from a lunch box. She watched with interest the gentle persuasion the man was using in feeding the woman. Once they finished their meal, he rushed to a nearby kiosk and brought a bottle of water. After the woman took a few sips, he helped her get up, and they walked towards the hospital building. Tonya watched until the couple was out of sight. She was moved by the man's concern.

It was almost noon, and soon her appointments would start, but she had no appetite for them. She needed time to think and analyze the situation in detail.

Tonya pressed the call bell and asked her assistant to push her appointments back by half an hour. Unless there was an emergency, she added, looking into her assistant's eyes to make sure that he understood her well. Tonya would never let an emergency case wait. Not even if her own life was at risk. Emergencies were emergencies. And even psychologists had emergency cases, however rare.

It took her exactly half an hour to clear her thoughts and revise the profile of the killer.

THE KILLER: *A ruthless, well-networked male. Young, about thirty, organized and focused. Emotionless, either due to a childhood trauma or a strong belief system. If the former, the killer is very educated. If the latter, he's a religious fanatic.*

She read it several times, cutting and adding words. The final form was near what she had thought initially. She emailed it to Vicks, then asked her assistant to start sending her patients in one by one.

CHAPTER 14

VICKS BOUGHT A new number from the shop adjacent to the café by showing his driving license. Even though the police would trace him eventually, he knew that they would still be trying to locate his position using his old number. The new phone would be operational in a few hours he was assured.

Minutes later he read Tonya's message on his laptop and shared his new number with her. He was on his way to the Welcome House Resort. This time his plan was to do something not in the rulebook. Desperate situations called for desperate measures. Not only did he need a booster for his investigative story, he wanted to be man enough to face the challenge head on. With a little preparation, he was confident he could cover a lot of ground.

He ducked down inside the auto-rickshaw when the vehicle passed the hotel. He had memorized the area well using Google maps and directed the rickshaw to take him to IINT Computer Institute, located half a kilometer north of the hotel.

He was wearing his golf cap pulled down over his face, just like on the morning he had visited the scene of the crime at Paharganj, to avoid being captured by any cameras. He got out at the institute's gate and paid the driver. Then he walked to a tea shop across the road and sat on a stool, surveying the scene around him. The place was crowded, which augured well for his plans. However, his area of focus was not the institute but the hotel. He waited for five minutes, then began walking along the road towards the hotel. It took him five more minutes to pass the imposing wrought iron gates of the Welcome House Resort. He glanced inside, just a single flick of his head, careful of the cameras he knew would be present in the vicinity of the gates. Vehicles were being searched, their hoods and trunks opened by security men. It was routine, and there was no need to be alarmed.

Vicks continued walking leisurely.

He reached the south side of the hotel's boundary and took the road to the left. After a couple of minutes, he took another left turn and walked for a few minutes more, which took him to the rear of the hotel. This was where he had to be careful and act quickly. He noticed a rickshaw and climbed into it. The driver pushed the meter down and asked, 'Sahib, where?'

'Just wait for a few minutes. We will go when my friend comes.'

The driver responded with a playful smile in the rearview mirror, but Vicks ignored him. He looked at his watch. The time was two p.m. The staff from the new shift must have taken over, and the old one should be on its way out any time now. He began to concentrate on the gate.

Though prepared, he was scared of seeing the security manager again. The red-eyed beast was dangerous, and had that staff member not interrupted, Vicks could have been dead meat by now. *How would they have disposed off my body?* He trembled and tried to change the direction of his thoughts.

He could see the hotel staff emerging from the gate. A few found their motorcycles on the roadside, kicked them to life, and went on their way, while others walked away from Vicks towards the bus stop. His eyes were searching for someone. Someone who could clear the fog that had clouded his mind and nearly got him killed. Vicks wanted his nerve back. He wanted to know the reason the security manager wanted him dead. He was desperate to pull back the curtain and find the dirty truth that was concealed behind it. He wanted answers.

After fifteen minutes, Vicks found a reason to smile. The man at the reception desk who had identified the pictures and given him information before the security manager interrupted was walking towards his motorcycle. He was alone. Vicks tapped on the driver's shoulder and asked him to follow the man on the motorcycle. The driver seemed uncertain but only for a second. Vicks knew the rickshaw drivers' true nature. They were privy to the underbelly of big cities: prostitution areas, gambling dens, drug havens. And for a little extra money, they invariably minded their own business.

'I will give you double the fare. Now hurry.'

The driver smiled in the rearview mirror and rolled his vehicle after the motorcycle. It was not easy to follow a motorcycle in an auto-rickshaw, but the man on the motorcycle was more disciplined than a regular biker. After a few kilometers of driving through tree-lined main roads, the motorcycle finally turned into a lane.

They had reached the old part of the city. The man on the motorcycle had no idea that he was being followed; he didn't turn his head even once. They meandered through a maze of narrow lanes, through the aroma of freshly tie-dyed clothes, fried *kachoris*, and cardamom tea. The turns sprang up every few meters, and men and women in colourful clothes milled about in small groups, feeding pigeons, tending to their paper kites, or loudly slurping their tea.

For a moment, Vicks thought of Tonya. As her face flashed through his mind, he smiled. In such a dense, peaceful amalgamation of colour and human tranquility, he thought of buying their home and starting a new life. Where neighbours could be invited from the window for tea and the sharing of fun and suffering was everyone's common agenda.

The motorcycle stopped, and the driver got off and removed his helmet. He looked up at a nearby two-story house, and Vicks' eyes followed his as the rickshaw came to a halt ten feet behind the motorcycle. A young woman waved through the metal grill of a small green window. The man raised his hand to respond. He was smiling. It was the smile of a man who had come home after a hard day's work.

Vicks paid the rickshaw driver and sent him away. Once he was finished here, he would walk to the main road and hire another. Hanging out with one person longer than necessary could create problems later.

The lady in the window disappeared as the man climbed the narrow stairs to the second-floor apartment. Vicks fell back a few more meters. He wanted to speak to the man but didn't know how. What if he raised an alarm and refused to cooperate? Or worse, what if the woman raised an alarm? Vicks would never be able to escape through these labyrinthine lanes; they would catch up with him in no time and hand him over to the Udaipur police.

After giving the couple ten minutes, Vicks walked up to their door. The plan was to adapt according to the situation. He could feel his heart beat like someone was tapping from inside his chest as he stood waiting after knocking gently on the door. The firing pin was, in any case, out of the grenade now, and there was no looking back. Vicks had no idea how the couple would react.

The door was opened by the lady. She smiled uncertainly. 'Yes?'

Though the man had worn a nametag when Vicks had spoken to him at the hotel, the subsequent events had happened so fast that he didn't remember his name. 'I am from the Welcome House Resort.'

'Oh, okay, please come in. Harish is in the bathroom; he will be with you in a moment.'

So far so good, thought Vicks, as he followed the lady into the house. There were two plastic chairs in the room they entered. He selected the one that put his back to the entrance.

He looked around. Rugs with elephants and camels printed on them hung from the walls, and a handmade carpet showing rabbits eating grass was under his feet. The room was ten by ten feet.

The lady brought him a glass of water. Vicks smiled and accepted it, took a few sips, and set it aside. When his eyes met hers, he smiled. The least he could do was to pretend to be a good visitor until the bomb exploded.

The unsuspecting man came into view a few seconds later, and the smile evaporated from his face as soon as he recognised Vicks.

CHAPTER 15

AMAR RATHORE SAT in his room at the Welcome House Resort, his forehead creased. Jamie was his friend, and Amar had enjoyed his hospitality numerous times over the last six months. Jamie had lots of money. But because he was rich, Jamie had explained to Amar, he had enemies too.

Jamie was staying at a private property not far from the Welcome House Resort that catered to super-rich western travelers seeking tranquility and the real Indian experience. Just two days ago, he had invited Amar to his room. That evening, when Amar arrived from his office, Jamie had seemed worried. He'd said upfront that he wanted Amar's help, help for which he was willing to compensate him handsomely.

Amar was immediately interested because he loved money. Only money could buy the pleasures that enhanced the joy of living. Like the finest alcohol, women, and drugs.

'My enemies are stalking me.' Jamie sipped Johnnie Walker Blue Label Whiskey and smiled at Amar.

'What can I do to help a friend?' asked Amar.

'Just be on the lookout for anyone who is asking about me. I mean... using my description, picture, etc.'

'Sure,' Amar said and refilled his own glass tumbler with Blue Label.

It was for this reason that, as soon as a man started asking the receptionist about Jamie, Amar, who'd been watching the CCTV feeds on the monitor in his office, called Jamie and informed him.

They had a short conversation. Amar had no idea why Jamie was scared of anyone asking about him. Therefore, he had been a wee bit apprehensive in the beginning, but when Jamie offered him two lakh rupees to kill the man, his hesitation was wiped clean by greed. Two hundred thousand was a lot of money.

But Amar was no fool, and this was not the first time he would kill a man. He knew the hazards of killing a stranger in a hotel. He could take care of the sound of the pistol by using a silencer, but he still had the challenge of disposing off the body. Smuggling the body out of the hotel was impossible, as all packages, including his, were checked thoroughly at the gates.

Amar's plan had been to scare the man with the pistol, then force him to drink a glass of water laced with sedatives. The glass sat in front of him even now. Once the man was unconscious, he could take him out of the hotel in his car under the guise of going to a hospital. From the hotel, his plan had been to drive to the highway and throw the unconscious man in front of a truck. He knew truckers in India never stopped when they hit a human body, dead or alive. Amar wanted to make it look like an accident.

But the woman and old man had walked in unexpectedly, ruining his plans. The target had escaped. Amar had been angry with himself, the loss of two lakh easy rupees spoiling his mood. He reached for the phone. 'Jamie, I am sorry; the man has escaped.'

'What? How?'

Amar explained the incident.

After he had finished, Jamie issued a warning that sent a chill along his spine: 'I don't accept such mistakes. You have to go.' The phone was disconnected.

Amar sat quietly, absorbing the danger he was in, and in the end, he smiled. The game was getting interesting. He knew Jamie would come after him. But could a foreigner really kill an Indian on his own turf?

He logged onto the hotel's website and removed his name, picture, and phone number, just in case. Next, he removed the picture of Jamie and his girlfriend, which he himself had taken, Julia Roberts smiling in the foreground. He copied this picture onto a pen drive and put it in his pocket. A man like Jamie, who was willing to kill to save himself, would present more problems for him later. This might become valuable insurance when the time came.

Amar had Jamie's girlfriend on his mind too. He knew they were in love, but he had not seen her for the last few days. When he asked Jamie about her, his eyes had widened for one heartbeat before he answered, 'She has gone and won't be returning anytime soon.'

It seemed weird that, though his lover had left, Jamie was biding his time in a foreign city without any apparent reason. But it was none of Amar's business, and he had given it no further thought. Until now.

Amar looked in the mirror and smiled. A plan was beginning to form in his mind. He knew where Jamie was staying. He admired the seriousness of his face in the mirror. It matched his state of mind. He wasn't prepared to let the two lakh rupees slip out of his hands. For his cocaine addiction, he needed two thousand rupees every other day, just to survive. His entire salary was used up in that. If he had more money, he could plan a trip to Goa for a few weeks, rooted in a five-star hotel with a trained Russian prostitute for pleasure. The red eyes in the mirror twinkled, and he sat down once again, facing the computer.

After sending an email to the General Manager of the hotel saying he was resigning effective immediately, Amar pocketed his pistol and walked out.

Chapter 16

JAMIE WAS NEARLY drunk. The information about Amar's failure had ignited a rare anger that he wasn't able to control. He dropped down on all fours and began to do pushups. After a hundred, sweating profusely, his eyes red and face flushed due to the labour and the alcohol, he straightened up.

Someone was looking for him. How could this have happened? When he had told Amar to watch for anyone the other evening, it was only to distract him from his concerned questions about Sherry Bing. Jamie had left no loose ends. No one had noticed him as he waited in front of the hotel. His disguise had been perfect, and he had left no clues in the room. Yet there was someone on his tail. Who could it be? Was it the police? Or Israeli intelligence? Amar had told him that the man was Indian and spoke good Hindi. So maybe it was the India collaborators of the Israeli intelligence service. It was time to make an important call. He took a long breath and dialed the number.

'I'm sorry, I'm sorry; I didn't intend to kill her.' He asked forgiveness after the voice on the other end shouted at him.

'Leave the city. How quickly can you erase all traces and get away?'

Jamie thought about Amar, the only person who

could cause trouble if he talked and complicate things further for him. After all, he had offered the man money to kill another human being. A minute later, he replied, 'In five to six hours, max.'

'Good. Do you know where to go?'

He said no, and the voice came back: 'Bangkok. You will pick up the tickets at the airport. The flight leaves at midnight. Hurry.'

After disconnecting, Jamie began to pack. For the first time in his life, he felt disillusioned with his employers, the Iranian intelligence service. He didn't like how they spoke to him. Was it his fault Sherry Bing had had nothing on her? He had searched her room thoroughly.

The memory of Sherry Bing increased his drunkenness, and he sat down on the bed heavily. He realized for the first time that, in pretending to be in love, he had actually fallen in love with her. How very much he wished she had not been a Jew. He clenched his fists, got up, and began to hit the wall. The pain brought tears to his eyes and his knuckles began to bleed, but he didn't stop.

And when he finally did, he felt determined to complete the task he'd been sent there to do. He had spent a lot of Iranian money on this operation. Sherry Bing was dead, and he could do nothing to make her alive again. He stared for a long time at the blood that had run down the wall and pooled on the floor.

His boss in Tehran was angry, and he had every right to be. After a couple more tumblers full of scotch,

Jamie redialed the number. This time, the voice on the other side was quiet as Jamie started to speak after a curt greeting. 'I have never failed, and I want to set this right. I beg you: give me one more chance.'

'Right. We are certain that she was waiting for her accomplice in that hotel. You shouldn't have killed her, even when you found nothing on her. I will try to get you back to base soon. But right now, you have to leave India. Make no mistakes this time.'

Jamie had no option but to believe the voice on the other end of the line. He had never met his boss. He had, in fact, never met anyone from Iranian intelligence. He had not even visited Tehran, except once, many years ago, to attend a wedding. He knew that, though he was a Muslim, living the life of a Christian had sullied his mind. He decided that after he completed this assignment, he would change all that. He would readopt his true name, Jalaluddin, grow a beard, wear a skull cap, and lead an alcohol-free life in the service of God. But the trouble was he was addicted to alcohol, and even to pork, which he had begun to relish, both prohibited in Islam. He was also used to not praying and had gone to only the Christian church as part of his cover.

The fact was, whether he liked it or not, Jamie was better off as a Christian. Though he loved the idea of being a Muslim—his ancestors had been the brave Persian warriors he had read so much about—he had covered too much ground in his life to change now. Christianity, like the evil religion it was, had poisoned his soul. Jamie's frustration multiplied, and he got on all fours once again to do more pushups.

He continued until he was confident that most of the alcohol had been sweated out. After quickly cleaning his room and packing his stuff, he spread a blanket over two spare pillows and quietly left the room, long-range binoculars in his hands. Instead of going to the reception desk, he climbed to the roof. One of the reasons he had booked a room in this hotel was because he liked the roof. From there, one could see anyone approaching from a long way off. No trees obstructed the view, and even at night, the lighting was good enough to keep watch. Jamie sat down to wait. He had a couple of hours before he left for the airport.

CHAPTER 17

'I MEAN NO harm to you, my friend.' Vicks kept his expression and voice as calm as he could.

The receptionist of the Welcome House Resort looked sharply at his wife, confusion on his face, and in his peripheral vision, Vicks saw her shrug.

'I mean you no harm,' Vicks repeated. 'Please sit down.'

'How did you know where I live?'

'I got your address from the hotel.'

'You are lying. The staff would never give it to anyone.'

'But they did give it to me.'

'They have my previous hostel address in their records. You followed me here, didn't you?'

Vicks nodded, took out his old business card, and identified himself as a correspondent of the *India Now* newspaper.

Harish appeared to relax a bit as he took the card from Vicks' extended hand and sat in the other chair. He nodded to his wife, who went away. Vicks strained his ears to hear a door open and shut, but nothing happened. The woman was not leaving the house in a panic to call for help. He was relieved. But she could call the police from inside the house. Vicks knew he would have to think fast and finish his business with this man quickly.

'Again, I am sorry to have arrived at your doorstep like this. But I wanted to know more about that man I showed you the photograph of.'

'As I told you before, he sometimes comes with his girlfriend for dinner at our restaurant. I don't know his name.'

'I saw his picture on your hotel's website after I left. But the picture was removed moments later. Why?'

A smile spread across Harish's face, which enhanced the jaggedness of the spikes in his hair. 'That's nothing strange. We often change the pictures, you know, refreshing our gallery. It's pretty standard for all hotels.'

'I agree. But only one picture was removed. The picture of the person I was looking for. I don't call that standard; I call it fishy.'

'Maybe a coincidence,' Harish offered.

'Removing just one picture and erasing the contact details and picture of your security manager simultaneously can't be a coincidence.' Vicks looked into his eyes.

'What do you mean?'

'You heard me right.' Vicks smiled and repeated his question about the missing picture. When Harish didn't say anything for a few seconds, Vicks continued, 'Did you know that your security manager was about to kill me in that room of his?'

Harish got to his feet. 'I think you must go now.'

'You don't have to be scared of Amar Rathore. Tell me more about him. I don't think he looked healthy. His eyes were distant, and he seemed to be possessed.'

'You must go now, or I will call the police.'

Vicks got to his feet too. But he wanted to give one final punch: 'That foreigner is a criminal. He has killed his girlfriend.'

'Are you sure?' The man's voice was uncertain.

'I would be lying if I said I was one hundred percent sure. But on the day his girlfriend was killed, that man was near the murder scene. I have a witness,' Vicks said, thinking of the tea cart seller.

Then he removed his phone and showed Harish the picture of the victim once more.

'Yes, it is her. Oh my God, she was so pretty, and they were so much in love, always kissing and cuddling. Why did he kill her?' He sat down again.

Vicks stayed standing. 'This man is a criminal. And so is Amar Rathore. Could you please find out more and help me with my investigation? I could give you—'

Harish cut him off. 'I don't want your money. I will see what I can do. But I will not be going to the office tomorrow.'

'Do something, please.'

The man called someone while Vicks waited. When he was done, he said, 'I have changed my shift for your sake. Please give me your number, and I will try to get information for you.'

'Thank you.' Vicks handed him a card on which he had scribbled his new number by hand and turned to leave but stopped when he heard Harish clear his throat behind him. He turned.

'My office has informed me that Amar has resigned. He is a dangerous person. We all keep our distance from him. Don't tell me later I didn't warn you.'

Vicks nodded and left the house without a word.

He walked for a few kilometers, keeping watch to be sure he was not being followed, and finally hopped into the next auto-rickshaw he saw.

CHAPTER 18

'WE NEED TO talk,' repeated Adam Shatner, the defense attaché to the Israeli ambassador to India.

Ariel Miller nodded and smiled as he got up from the lawn. 'No talking before I get coffee and some bamba.' The embassy ought to have it; it was a popular Israeli snack.

'Of course.'

They crossed the lawn and walked into the gated embassy. For the next half hour, while Ariel gorged on a plateful of the high-calorie bamba and slurped coffee without a care in the world, Adam waited patiently. Finally, Ariel wiped his lips, burped and looked up.

'I am sorry,' Adam said, 'I—'

Ariel cut him off with a wave of his hand, urging him to get to the point straightaway.

'Tel Aviv has briefed us about you. So I know who you are, Mr. Secret Agent. But I still have one question. What is your business in India?'

'Okay, first of all, thanks for the hospitality,' Ariel smiled, meaning the expression, as another burp wriggled up his esophagus, embarrassing him this time. 'I am sure you know that I can't answer all your questions.' After Adam nodded, he said, 'I have important spy business here. Now, can you tell me who killed Sherry Bing?'

'What is your business with her?'

'I can't tell you that.'

Adam shrugged his shoulders, bringing them up to stop squarer than before. At the same time, his eyebrows straightened and his mouth turned into a pencil-thin line that twitched. After a few seconds of silence, he spoke, clearly agitated. 'Come on, I am the defense attaché to the ambassador, Ariel, not some embassy clerk. I am a colonel in the Israeli Army... You've got to tell me a bit more. I know how to handle information.'

'Fair enough. I have something I wanted to give to Sherry. But she is dead because you locked me in that bloody safe house of yours.' Ariel's voice rose without his intending it to. He took a deliberate breath, turned his head away to fight the moisture that had started to shimmer in his eyes, and continued, staring out the window, his voice now just a whisper. 'She waited for me for two days, but someone got wind of it and eliminated her.'

'I am sorry for her death but not sorry for arresting you.'

'Now I know you are from the army.' Ariel chuckled.

Adam got the hint and sulked but didn't react. They sat quietly for some time, not looking at each other, while Israeli Prime Minster Benjamin Netanyahu looked on from the wall behind them.

Now that Ariel had eaten, his brain began to process the information he had collected. Anger and frustration were replaced with clever thinking. After ten minutes, he looked up at Adam and asked him for a secure telephone connection to place a call. He was escorted to a room at the end of a long corridor with people working in cubicles on either side. Once he was in the room, he was left alone. Adam closed the door and said he would wait outside in the corridor.

Ariel emerged after five minutes. He had gotten his anticipated course of action authorized by the higher command at Mossad headquarters. Once settled into the briefing room again, Ariel took out the letter that had been intended for Sherry Bing and gave it to Adam without a word. Adam opened the paper, peered at it for a few seconds, then shrugged. 'What does this mean?'

'Please scan it and email it using your encryption software.'

'Email it to whom?'

Ariel picked up a piece of paper and a pen from the table, scribbled an email address, and gave it to him.

'And?'

'This paper is all I've got. It came from someone who was under deep cover in Tehran, someone who was killed when his identity was compromised. The man was Sherry Bing's father. There is important information in there, something that we need.'

'But the words don't mean anything. Unless we have the code, I am afraid we can't understand the message,' Adam waved the paper at him. Ariel had never seen a stupider person. The colonel was just reading the writing on the wall, stating the obvious. It was no wonder, given the guy was from the army, Ariel mused, and smiled at his thought.

'We are discussing an important matter here, and you are smiling.'

'Come on, General,' Ariel teased. 'I know what is in it. I gave it to you, remember?'

Adam walked out of the briefing room. The manner in which he slammed the door suggested that he was angry. Ariel smiled. It was good to be back.

The years that had gone by had mellowed his anger at himself for being so ugly. In fact, he didn't consider himself ugly anymore. The woman he'd had an affair with back in Tehran had said many times that he was handsome. Even if she had just gotten carried away because he gave her a lot of money in exchange for sex, it made him realize that reaching his thirties had diluted his ugliness. His face had filled in, which made his nose seem less obvious, and the pimples were now covered by a thick beard.

When he'd called Tel Aviv, they ordered him to send the paper straightaway. They had invented a machine recently, they said, called an alphabet scrambler, which scrambled the twenty-six letters of the English alphabet at super-high speed, and as the words began to make sense, the machine laid them out in sequence.

Now all Ariel had to do was wait for further instructions. Perhaps it was just an emotional letter from a father to his daughter that the father had wanted to keep private. If that was the case, it would be very wrong for Ariel and his agency to invade their privacy. There was another possibility, though. It could be something of significance to Israel's security. But if it was indeed something of national importance, surely the old man would have just told him instead of writing it down in a coded message to his daughter.

The thought stayed with him for a while. This was an important question, and he didn't want to rush to any conclusion. In any case, the scrambling machine would figure it out soon enough. He clung to that hope for the moment.

A man looked into the briefing room and announced, 'Sir, I have been directed to escort you to your room.'

'Of course.'

'Luggage?' the man asked, looking around the room.

'None.' He got up.

Ariel followed the man out of the administration block. They walked around a fountain, passed a lawn bordered with roses and gerberas, and finally entered a three-story building.

There was no lift, so they climbed the stairs past the first two floors. The third floor had six doors, arranged three on either side of the corridor. The man paused, looked at Ariel, and smiled before opening the first door on the right.

The room was big and opened into another room. It was a suite, elegantly furnished. Ariel thanked the man, and as soon as he was alone, he slid into the bed. He was so drowsy from tiredness and the excessive food he had eaten that he started to snore lightly in less than ten seconds.

CHAPTER 19

JAMIE SMILED WHEN he saw Amar Rathore come into view. The prey was walking towards the hunter. It gave him a high, and the pleasure made him dizzy. At that moment, another killing was exactly what he needed to lift his spirits.

Amar was behaving exactly as he had hoped. Through his binoculars, he saw Amar stop about two hundred meters short of the entrance to Jamie's hotel. Amar had assumed that the naked eye would not be able to see him that far away. But he had been foolish. He had no idea that Jamie, with his powerful 25X digital binoculars, was better prepared.

He had never liked Amar. Addicted to drugs and women, the bastard was a slimy sonofabitch. He was overconfident about his abilities and had created a mess for Jamie by pointing a gun at a stranger and not killing him. Now, that stranger, whoever he was, must be better preparing himself. Jamie regretted asking Amar to kill him.

If Jamie wanted to, he could have ignored Amar's mistake. Just gotten the hell out of India. The prospect of reaching Bangkok was already calming his nerves. But Jamie was trained not to spare those who failed in their assignments.

As Amar stepped onto a side road and began nearing the hotel, keeping away from the main road leading to the hotel's entrance, Jamie exhaled. It would all be over in less than an hour. For him, killing was a pleasure better than sex. The idea of one human completely conquering another was exhilarating. It was a perfection that nature had created. There was nothing abnormal about killing. Even in the animal kingdom, the powerful killed the weak. And if Amar turned out to be more powerful and intelligent than him, Jamie would be happy to die.

'It's all about power,' his mentor, a mullah at the mosque in the suburbs of London that Jamie frequented as a young adult, used to say. 'The day is not far off when our Muslim brothers will prove to all the infidels in the world that Muslims are the most powerful.'

Jamie liked the idea of propagating the faith he was born in. It gave meaning to his existence. He liked the fact that Muslims were disciplined. Men and women had clearly defined roles. There were no overlaps. Life was good. There was no scope for anything unnatural, like gays, which many of the Christians seemed to be okay with. Their weak religion had made them confused. He vowed that he wouldn't let that happen to his fellow Muslims.

Therefore, when he was about twenty, he had said to the mullah after Friday prayers, 'I want to spread the message of Islam. I want to save the world.'

The mullah had smiled divinely, patted his back, and asked him to come the next morning. As soon as

Jamie arrived the next day, he was taken to a secret room inside the mosque where three others were waiting. Their lectures over the next three hours convinced him beyond any doubt that this was the best decision of his life.

Jamie's mother opposed his going for training two months later, but his father said he was proud of him. Their son was doing something that he couldn't. And his mother, like a dutiful Muslim wife, had not disagreed with her husband. She smiled and wished him luck. Jamie was not entirely certain she did so happily, but that didn't matter. It was a masculine responsibility, and she had no role to play in it.

During training at a secret location in Turkey, it had been explained to him that, for the good of Islam, every method of warfare was acceptable. He was taught how to become a spy. Lessons in surveillance, survival, methods of torture, and the use of weapons were taught to him over the next three years. He was also trained to live like a westerner so it would be easy for him to blend in when the time came. From drinking alcohol to eating all kinds of meat and praying in a church, he was exposed to the lifestyle of his adversaries. When his training was over, he was assigned a boss who explained his first assignment. As 'Jamie' in India, he was required to woo and extract information from a Jewish girl called Sherry Bing.

Everything had been going to plan until he was forced to kill Sherry Bing. And now there were Amar's phone calls, the first to tell Jamie that someone was looking for him all over town with a sketch in his hands, and the second to say that Amar had failed to kill that man. Jamie knew that this was a minor lapse, one which he was confident of correcting soon. Though this act would be outside the scope of his assignment, he was convinced of its need, as he had cultivated Amar for something in which the man had failed, and therefore, punishment was inevitable.

Jamie thought of the covered pillows under the blanket in his room, arranged to give the illusion of someone sleeping in the bed. On the side table, there was a glass tumbler and an unfinished bottle of Johnnie Walker Blue Label whiskey.

Jamie walked across the roof and sat down to wait for his prey.

CHAPTER 20

VICKS WAS SIPPING tea and eating pakoras at a wayside stall in Udaipur when he received Harish's call.

'Is this Vicks Menon?'

'Yes.'

'You sound different. Are you the same journalist I met this morning?'

'Harish...' Vicks had identified his voice. 'I am sorry, I was eating... Okay, give me a sec... Can you make out my voice now?'

'Yes... Okay, I have the information about the man you were looking for. His name is Jamie, and his address is...' He told him and Vicks noted it down.

Vicks couldn't believe his luck. 'That was quick. Thank you very much, but how did you get the details so fast?'

'I changed my work shift, like I said I would. I'm at the hotel now, and I got it from my sources in the luxury resorts industry. But this is all I have. Another thing, the man is British.'

'Thank you very much.' Vicks meant every word.

'By the way, you mentioned that picture of Jamie and his girlfriend... the one that was later deleted from our website. I was successful in digging it up, and I've just emailed it to the address on the card you gave me. Got to go now.' Vicks heard the click in his ear even before he could respond. But now he had what he needed. This was surely the jackpot.

He took out his laptop and checked Google maps for Jamie's address. Vicks was just five kilometers from the hotel where his target was holed up. Things were beginning to gel at last, and he was hot on the killer's trail. There was not a moment to lose. He accessed his email account and downloaded the picture Harish had sent of Jamie and Sherry Bing, with Julia Roberts in the foreground. He paused a moment to look at the demure Sherry Bing, victim of a mindless killing, and felt a pang of pain. She had been executed effortlessly, and yet with so much care. He took a deep breath and locked his gaze on the picture of Jamie. There was a wild intensity in the man, as if fear was camouflaged by overconfidence. Something that reminded Vicks of his father. He was stumped by the sudden comparison and admonished himself silently.

During the next half hour, Vicks made a plan. A foolproof plan. Going straight to the killer's hotel was too dangerous. He was unarmed, but the killer was not. A criminal who had people like Amar snooping for him would have an advance warning system in place. No doubt about it.

Vicks wanted to exploit that. The idea was to use the enemy's own trap to capture him. After some more thought, the plan solidified in his mind.

It was time to make the call. 'Boss. I've found the killer. His name is Jamie. He is a British national. I am attaching his picture, taken with the victim in happier times.'

'How sure are you?'

'One hundred percent. Remember, I was the first person to see the dead woman. The woman in the picture *is* her. I'd bet my career on this. Period.'

'Okay. Just email it to me. So what's your plan now?'

'I want to find out why this Jamie character killed her.'

'That's for the police to decide.'

'An investigative reporter is sometimes a policeman in disguise.' Vicks disconnected the phone. It was the first time he'd ever had the last word with his boss. It made him smile. But he knew his boss would call him back. Vicks looked at his phone for a long time, but it remained silent.

CHAPTER 21

THE SMILE VANISHED from Jamie's face as he watched, from his perch on the rooftop, as Amar dropped softly down onto the back lawn of the hotel. A camera covered that area, but Jamie knew nobody watched the monitor. The camera had been installed more for deterrence than any serious surveillance. Probably because the likelihood of trespassers was rare and the walls were high enough to deter any prospective thieves. Though evidently not high enough for Amar.

Amar had turned up in green-and-brown camouflage army fatigues. Had he been in the army? Jamie's worry intensified. But it embedded the challenge of killing his adversary that much deeper. The exhilaration multiplied, and Jamie's existence as a spy-on-the-job got a shot in the arm.

Four floors below, Amar pussyfooted over and paused right under Jamie's position, his back pressed against the wall. Jamie watched him remove his pistol from his jacket and screw a silencer on the barrel. Jamie couldn't see his face and eyes, but he noticed that his movements were measured.

Amar looked up. It was sudden, totally unexpected, and Jamie jumped back instinctively, his heart racing. Had Amar seen him, or had he ducked in the nick of time? If Jamie's position had been compromised, it would be a huge tactical loss. But there was no time left to deliberate on the ifs or buts.

Jamie climbed down from the roof, making as little sound as he could, and waited at the top of the stairs a floor above his room. He crouched like a tiger moments before the attack, his senses heightened. In one hand Jamie held a pistol and in the other a six-inch knife.

After a few minutes, he heard soft footsteps. A drop of sweat slithered down his forehead and came to rest on the tip of his nose. It was the anticipation of the kill, the imminent decimation of another human being, the smell of victory. He couldn't hear the key turn in the lock, but the slow whine of the door as it swung open was discernable. Bent over, he walked down the stairs like a predator and crouched next to the open door to wait.

Jamie was in the most dangerous phase of the hunt. Amar was armed and well-trained, as his army fatigues suggested. It would be a close-combat battle. And Jamie knew that in all close-combat battles, guts and instinct played a major role. He imagined the room, placed his enemy in the most probable position inside, and waited. A moment later, he heard three soft plops. Now was the time.

He walked into the room on his toes, slowly, and when he saw Amar's back, stopped and spoke. 'You shouldn't have done that, my friend.'

Amar swung around. His right hand moved wildly as it tried to point the gun in the direction of the sound. But the reflex was a second late. Or perhaps just a fraction of a second. Jamie threw his knife, which pierced Amar's neck through and through, puncturing the windpipe and slicing his jugular. As Amar fell, the gun fired into the ceiling.

Amar's left hand lifted, trying to stop the bleeding; the pistol fell from the other hand as a result of shock and pain, and it reached for the neck too. But the blood continued to flow. The harder he tried, the faster it gushed out, and as the panic of death drew near, the flow increased even more.

Jamie kicked the pistol away and looked down at the sprawled man. He pulled a chair over and sat next to him. His head was spinning, the effects of winning making him dizzy. He looked at Amar and got his control back in a few seconds.

Jamie picked up his glass from the side table and filled it with scotch as Amar lay on the floor, trying to stop the blood loss. He took a sip and smiled. 'Want a drink, my friend?'

Amar tried to speak, and the blood found a new exit through his mouth. He quickly shut it, his eyes getting even redder and his body shaking with fear, as it knew what came next.

'You made it easier for me by walking in here, Amar. What did you think, that I was some amateur?' Jamie smiled at Amar's inability to answer and continued. 'Now I will leave you here in this room. By the look of your wound, I think you will slip into a coma in a few minutes and die in your sleep. I am sorry, but you see, I can do nothing for you. I have to get on a plane to Bangkok to screw some real good pussies. Goodbye.'

Jamie had decided against killing him outright. He wanted Amar to experience the pain; he wanted him to pay a price for his failure. The added bonus was that one more infidel had been removed from the earth.

He picked up his bags and went down to the reception desk. A man with a narrow face, who he had seen earlier, smiled in greeting.

'My girlfriend is still in my room. Please add the rent for another day to my bill. She will leave tomorrow morning. She's tired, so please don't disturb her.'

'Of course, sir,' the receptionist said with a bow, trained not to ask uncomfortable questions to the rich and famous tourists who frequented the heritage property.

Jamie refused the hotel's complimentary airport service and instead walked out on his own after paying his bill, dragging his suitcase out to the road. He climbed into an auto-rickshaw, changed to a different one after a kilometer, and reached the airport an hour before the scheduled departure time. He was happy with what he had achieved so far, and the pain of not having found anything on Sherry Bing had dulled a little. There was someone looking for him in Udaipur, but in a few hours, he would be out of India, so there was nothing to worry about anymore.

He smiled, but it didn't last more than a few seconds. Now that he was finally leaving the city he had shared with Sherry Bing, his lover, he was filled with an uncomfortable nostalgia that made his body shake.

Chapter 22

ARIEL WOKE WITH a start. The comfort of the guest room in the Israeli embassy had put him to sleep, but no sooner had his body shaken off its tiredness, his mind awoke. He sat up, wondering for a moment where he was. Not used to such a comfortable room after the last five years, it took him a minute to figure it out.

Finally, he pulled the blanket away, smiled into the small camera in the flower vase on the side table, and wandered into the kitchenette to brew some coffee. After a minute, cup in hand, he walked to the window, slid the curtains on one side, and looked out. The green of the lawns soothed his eyes. The coffee brightened the green some more as he took a few sips. His brain began to emerge from under the gray darkness of sleepiness.

With his coffee finished, he sat down to think. The death of Sherry Bing and Ariel's inability to pass her father's message to the young woman bit him hard.

But he knew he could do nothing about it now. It was time to move on. Death, or the escape from it, was part and parcel of an intelligence operative's life. A spy's occupational hazard. He had chosen this career of his own volition. But Sherry had had nothing to do with the intelligence service. She was what the Americans called collateral damage. Someone caught in the crossfire. Just too bad.

Though he was satisfied with his own reasoning and logic, he felt an unbalanced sway of emotion within him.

He thought of the Iranian prostitute he'd visited on the weekends. She'd genuinely liked him; he could feel it. He felt like a man in her arms; he felt strong and alive as he shoved into her late at night. She was an enemy, yet her eyes told a different story whenever the time came for him to leave. Was he in love with her, the woman who'd had sex with so many others, all Iranians, all Muslims, all enemies of his land? These things were too complex to understand, and he decided, with a wave of frustration, not to let his thoughts wander back to the past.

He picked the local newspaper up off the table, discovered it was the previous day's paper, and began to read the story of Sherry Bing. The police had confirmed that they had a few leads. Like that the killer came from the state of Rajasthan. Adam had already told him about it.

Who had killed Sherry Bing? A jaded lover? A thief? An enemy?

He pushed the thought away. Who killed Sherry and why was none of his business. It was the business of the embassy. The embassy protected their citizens who came to visit India. Perhaps he would be ordered to return to Tel Aviv soon. He got up, lay back down on the bed, and closed his eyes in a half-sleep. The feeling of being in a safe place, away from all danger, soothed his edginess. It felt like home.

There was someone outside. Ariel opened his eyes and looked at the clock. He must have napped for about an hour. He opened the door, and Adam Shatner came charging in like a bull on business.

'Ariel, you will not believe this!'

'What?'

'The message from Sherry Bing's father has been decoded.'

'Oh! So?'

Adam looked around the room, walked to the bathroom to check, opened the closet and stuck his head inside, and finally, when he was satisfied that there was no one else in the room, he whispered, 'It contains very sensitive information.'

'Sensitive? From a father to his daughter? You must be kidding.'

'No, I am not.'

'Okay, so what is it?'

'They haven't told me that.' And he sat on the bed, his expression suggesting frustration.

Ariel took the chair opposite and said, 'Assume for the moment that I choose to agree with you. Please tell me why our own spy would give me a secret message for our government via his daughter. And in a code known only to her. He could have given it straight to me.'

Adam thought for a while, then said, his voice once again a whisper, 'Because he suspected that, if you were caught and tortured, the enemies would get the message from you.'

It made sense and was something that had crossed Ariel's mind too. He stretched and smiled at Adam.

Adam smiled back. 'They want you on the phone in half an hour. Please come to the ambassador's office. Calls to that number use a technology that ensures that if the phone is tapped, the voices sound continuously garbled.'

Adam left, closing the door behind him rather loudly. Army guys, mused Ariel, always in a hurry, even if they don't know what they are hurrying for. He thought it to amuse himself, but a smile didn't come to his face. His sharp brain had already started working out the probabilities of what lay ahead.

CHAPTER 23

'MADAM, THE POLICE are here.' It was Tonya's assistant, peering into her office.

'After this patient, please. Can you ask them to wait?' She turned to the middle-aged woman seated opposite her and said, her voice professional, 'Please continue.'

Before the woman could speak, a man in a khaki uniform entered the office, followed by the harried-looking assistant. 'Sir, you can't just push your way in—'

Tonya raised her hand to stop her assistant. The policeman glared at him, but when he turned to look at Tonya, his expression changed. 'I am sorry, doctor, but this is about a murder, and it can't wait.'

She nodded and asked her assistant to take the old woman out. After the two of them had left, she turned her gaze to the policeman, who had seated himself in a chair.

'My name is Rao Sachin, and I'm an Assistant Commissioner with the Delhi Police. We are investigating the murder of a foreign national in Paharganj. I am sure you must have read about it.' He paused, removed his peaked cap and placed it on the table between the two of them, scratched his chin, and continued, 'I am here to ask you where your boyfriend, Vicks Menon, is.'

'You could have just called me instead of taking the trouble to come all the way here. An ACP in my office; what an honour.'

'Where is he?' He looked straight into her eyes.

Tonya knew that if she told him, the police would unleash all their dogs on Vicks. Vicks had told her about *The Vortex*. She felt sorry for him, so she decided to mislead the police. That would give Vicks more time to unravel the mystery surrounding the murder. 'We have separated and are no longer in a relationship. I have no idea where he is.'

'Is he not in touch with you?' The policeman smiled viciously now.

His smile was upsetting. Though pleasant in his manners and handsome, he was still a policeman, and the rawness was evident. Did he know about her conversations with Vicks? 'No.'

'Okay, if he calls you, tell him he is in a lot of trouble.' ACP Rao Sachin got to his feet and left without waiting for Tonya to react. Not that she had anything to say.

Tonya drank some water and tried to concentrate. Vicks was using a new phone, so it was practically impossible for the police to track him down.

Yet she knew she had to warn him. Tonya looked at her cell phone but couldn't risk using it to call Vicks. If her phone was being monitored, calling Vicks now could reveal his new number. Perhaps the landline? But they could be monitoring the landline too.

Her assistant looked in and asked if she was ready to resume with the old lady.

'Give me five minutes.' Tonya walked out of her consultation room and headed to the doctors' restroom. On the way, she saw an office with its door ajar. She pushed it open. There was no one in the room. She entered quietly, picked up the phone on the table, and dialed Vicks' new number.

'Vicks,' she began as soon as he answered, her voice just a whisper, 'the police came to my office. They wanted to know where you are.'

'Okay, I was expecting this. But what is this number you're calling from? Are you okay?'

'Yes, I'm fine. I'm calling from someone else's office, in case the police have my phone tapped and are listening.'

'I get it now. Please don't worry. Don't give them my number, and if they pressure you and you have to, please hold on until tonight. Keep them guessing. I will change my number again tonight. I love you.'

The sudden change of emotion threw her off. He stayed on the line, obviously hoping for her to respond, his breathing loud in her ear. The suddenness of her need to call hadn't prepared her for this. 'I've got to go now,' she said, like she was in a hurry, and hung up.

It was rude not to respond, and Vicks was in danger; the least she could do was soothe his nerves by telling him how she felt about him. All she had to do was speak the truth. But sometimes, speaking the truth is not an easy thing to do.

Tonya returned to her office and was shocked to see ACP Rao seated there. He had a smirk on his face. 'Thank you!' was all he said. Tonya was left bewildered about what he was thanking her for.

Then she understood. He had never left. They'd expected her to call, and stupidly, that was exactly what she did. They'd left that office door open as a trap for her, and she'd fallen right into it. 'Please go away. I am a doctor, and I have work to do.'

He got to his feet and walked out, but turned at the door, 'The next time you assist someone the police are looking for, I will get an arrest warrant issued. Are we clear?'

She nodded weakly and stared at the closed door for a long time.

CHAPTER 24

VICKS CHECKED AND rechecked the website of the *India Now* newspaper. He refreshed it many times, but the contents remained the same. The picture of Jamie and the murdered woman that he had emailed to his boss had not been published yet. More than two hours had elapsed, and he was left wondering why his boss was delaying.

He decided against calling him. Perhaps in another hour, he might have more information. Vicks now knew where Jamie lived, and if he took precautions, he might soon find out more details.

Vicks reached the heritage property and paused to watch the entrance, wondering how best to approach. Walking straight in was risky. He could be attacked. For criminals like Jamie, killing was part of the daily existential grind. It was routine. No pangs of guilt to deal with, just a job done.

Vicks thought of the few policemen he knew in Delhi. One was a Station House Officer who'd gone to college with him and another was a Joint Commissioner of the Delhi police, to whom he was related on his mother's side. The Delhi police had picked up his trail. He'd known they had to, sooner or later.

Tonya was under surveillance too. Were they already in Udaipur? It was possible, as he'd used his old phone late last night. By tracking his number, they could easily reach the hotel he'd stayed in last night. But Udaipur was a big city, and he had not left any evidence in his room of where he would be during the day. And they didn't know his new number. Tonya had used good presence of mind in calling and warning him from an unrelated number. So tracking him was out of the question.

Vicks saw a man emerge from the hotel dragging a suitcase. Acting on instinct, he hid behind a peepal tree off to one side. The man drew close, and when he was about fifty feet away, Vicks knew who he was. It was Jamie, Sherry Bing's killer. He seemed to be at ease, his gait normal, even carefree. The murderer had checked out of his hotel and was on his way somewhere.

Vicks had investigated many stories for his newspaper. He had been to countless crime scenes, met many criminals in jail, and been to courtrooms to watch the police investigations and the pronouncements of guilty and not guilty. But never in his life had he been left confounded like this.

He couldn't just walk up to the man and ask him questions. Jamie would either kill him or just stare and walk away. He had no leverage to convince the killer that he had to talk to him. What he was trying to do was actually the job of the police. He thought of dialing 100 but decided against it.

Vicks stood there, distressed, thinking about his lack of power, as the killer passed his position, got into an auto-rickshaw, and said something to the driver.

Vicks strained to hear what he was saying, but the roar of the engine drowned it out. A moment later, the rickshaw drove off.

He stepped out of cover, scratching his head and looking after the departing vehicle. It was only a speck now. Vicks hurried into the hotel.

The receptionist had an exceptionally narrow face. He had distant eyes; eyes that wouldn't see beyond what was necessary. The kind of eyes hotel receptionists looking for a serious job with the rich and famous have. 'Yes, sir?'

'The man who just walked away. Was that Mr. Jamie?'

'Sir, our clients' confidentiality is important to us. I can tell you nothing. Are you with the police?'

Vicks lost his cool. He bent forward, pulled the man towards him by his tie, and hissed, 'The key to the room he was in. Now.'

The man froze. Vicks repeated the order with extra steel in his voice. There was a camera on top of the reception desk, and he expected someone to barge in at any moment.

The receptionist reached his hand behind him and pulled out a key. Extending his hand, he said, his voice wavering with fear, 'Sir, what you're doing is illegal.'

Vicks snatched the key, saw the number on it, and ran up the stairs. The room was on the second floor. He opened the door and walked in, the door banging against the wall. There was no need to take any precautions, as he had seen the killer walking away. Halfway into the room, Vicks came to a halt. There was a man on the floor in a pool of blood.

Slowly, he walked closer to the man on the floor, taking pictures as he went, careful not to step in the trails of blood that were snaking towards the door. The man's face was turned the other way. Vicks jumped over him to look.

It was Amar, his eyes as red as the blood around him. There was no need to check whether he was dead. There was a wound in his neck, his hands clasped around it. He must have tried desperately to stop the bleeding.

Vicks heard a commotion behind him. It was the receptionist, his hand over his mouth, with another person about his age standing solemnly beside him.

'Call the police. Jamie has done this to him. Hurry.'

Vicks walked out. Perhaps it was time to call in the Delhi police. He emailed a picture of the dead Amar to his boss, then called and quickly narrated the incident over the phone. After he had finished updating him, Vicks said, 'Boss, the Delhi police are on my back. I need your help... Please tell them that all I was doing was investigating a story for the newspaper.'

'Sure, I will. But where is the killer?'

'I know where he is. But I want one lakh rupees deposited into my account.'

After his boss agreed, Vicks told him what Amar had written in blood on the floor: Bangkok.

'So that means the others will have seen it too?'

'No boss, I sent them away to call the police, and before I left, more blood had run over it.'

'Smart. So you remain hot on the killer's heels. Good. I will post the new details right now and our website hits will go through the roof. I'll be doubling our advertisers' rates after this story.'

Vicks wanted to hang up, but stayed calm and pocketed his phone only after his boss finally disconnected.

CHAPTER 25

VICKS CALLED INSPECTOR Mohan Gandhi, the head of the Munirka police station in Delhi, his college friend. It was time to take some drastic measures.

'Hi Vicks, how are you?'

'I'm fine... Look, I'm doing a story on that Paharganj murder.'

'Yeah, okay. That story is hot these days.'

'The thing is, I was the first to reach the crime scene, but I didn't share anything with the police. Now they suspect me of foul play and are looking for me. They're looking for a scapegoat, and I fit their needs perfectly. As you know, I lost my job, so I was just trying to go the extra distance to get a good story.'

'I think you might be in a lot of trouble, my friend. What do you want me to do?'

'Suggest something that will get the police off my back for a few days so I can continue investigating the story.' He sounded desperate. But Gandhi was a close friend, someone he could trust and talk to without any pretense.

'I don't think I'll be able to suggest anything, because from what I heard, the case is being handled by the intelligence service.'

'Why Intelligence?'

'Rumour has it that the murder was just the tip of the iceberg, and there's a lot underneath. I think that, as we speak, resources are being mobilized for a massive manhunt. If you give yourself up, it will save you a lot of trouble, Vicks.'

'What about my story? My job?'

'What use will your job be if they arrest you and put you behind bars? If this case takes a national security direction, you are fucked for good, my friend. Give yourself up and tell them your side of the story. You have nothing to hide.'

For a moment, Vicks was enraged; it felt like he was talking to a stranger, not a friend. But he swallowed hard and thanked Gandhi, promising that he would think about giving himself up.

It took him two minutes to decide. As he stepped out of the hotel, two policemen passed him. They were in khakis, DP on their shoulder flaps, which stood for Delhi Police. The receptionist had informed the police of the murder just a minute ago, and the police were already there. Not the Udaipur police, who should have responded to the 100 call, but the Delhi police. Vicks continued walking, expecting them to call him back. But they didn't, and when he thought he was a reasonable distance away, he began to run.

The murderer would try to get away. The question was, which route would he take? The quickest way out was by plane, but to fly to Bangkok, he'd have to get to Delhi or Mumbai. He wouldn't take a bus, as it would take eleven hours to reach Delhi, during which time, if the police got wind of the murder, they would erect road blocks. Trains were slower too and, in addition, erratic. A foreigner would stand out on a bus or train in any case. Taking a taxi would save a couple of hours but the trouble of roadblocks remained.

Vicks hailed a passing auto-rickshaw. As soon he was settled in, he logged into his laptop to check flights to Bangkok from Delhi and Mumbai in the next five to ten hours. There wasn't a flight out of Mumbai for the next twelve hours, but there was one from Delhi in six hours. The real trouble was the flight from Udaipur to Delhi. There was one leaving in forty-five minutes, and the airport was still twenty minutes away. Vicks bought a ticket using his credit card, then called the airline's number and pleaded with them to hold the plane, adding that he had to get to Delhi for a family emergency. They said they would wait an extra five minutes for him.

Vicks urged the auto-rickshaw driver to go faster. The driver said okay, and the vehicle started to swerve dangerously, negotiating the heavy evening traffic. Vicks held his breath. What he was doing was dangerous. He had no option but to have faith in the driver. Finally, he could see the airport in the distance. He would make it in the nick of time.

His phone began to buzz in his pocket. He dug it out and looked at the screen. The flashing number began with the telephone code for the city of Udaipur.

'Hello?'

'Sir, I am calling from the airport. Where are you? The boarding is done, and the captain has asked twice for permission to taxi. We can't hold the plane any longer.'

'Madam, I can see the airport from my auto-rickshaw. It will just take me five more minutes. Please.'

'I will try, but it is difficult.' She hung up.

As the rickshaw skidded to a halt at the airport, Vicks thrust a hundred-rupee note into the driver's hand to cover the cost of the journey, picked up his shoulder bag, and ran inside. At the gate, he jumped the line and pleaded with the CISF security guard to let him pass. After Vicks was let inside, he ran to the check-in counter, once again jumped the queue, and announced his flight number.

'I am sorry, sir, you are too late. The aircraft has taxied and is already lined up for takeoff.'

'Please stop it... I have an emergency.' He wished he could just tell them that there was a killer on board. Even though he was not hundred percent sure, the chance of Jamie being on board the aircraft was almost certain, as this was the only flight that would reach Delhi in time to make the Bangkok flight.

The lady at the check-in counter shrugged. 'Sorry, I can't do anything. But you could try speaking to the airport manager.' She pointed towards the opposite side of the room.

Vicks ran towards the airport manager's office. As he ran, he could see the aircraft lined up through the window. But there was no one in the office. He wiped the sweat from his face and looked out the window as the aircraft began to roll down the runway to take off. There was nothing he could do now.

'Are you looking for me?'

Vicks heard the door close behind him and turned to face the airport manager.

The man who stood before him was the last person he had expected to see. Vicks tried to speak, but no words came out.

Standing in front of him was Jamie.

CHAPTER 26

JAMIE HAD SEEN a man run into the airport. As a spy, he knew how to plan for contingencies, and one was staring at him right at that moment. He knew from the stranger's behavior that he was desperate to board the plane. But who was this man? Jamie had no way of knowing. Perhaps the man was looking for him? Perhaps not. In any case, Jamie had just committed a crime, and though the chances of it being discovered before he flew out were remote, he could not ignore any abnormality around him.

He waited for the stranger to speak at the check-in counter, hiding behind a newspaper he wasn't reading. When the man started to move towards the airport manager's office, Jamie followed him, keeping a distance of about twenty feet. The man entered the office, and Jamie peeped inside. There was no one else inside. As the man turned to look out the window of the airport manager's office at the plane taxiing on the runway, Jamie stepped inside and closed the door gently.

This was the tricky part. He had disposed off his knife and pistol in a roadside dustbin on the way to the airport. There was no way he could take any weapons on a plane. And he knew replacement gear would be waiting for him once he arrived in Bangkok. But at the moment, he had only his bare hands to take care of the situation. And he knew his bare hands were good enough. So there was nothing to worry.

If the man recognized Jamie, his expression would show it. If he was someone who genuinely wanted to get on that plane, he would look through him and ask something like, 'Are you the airport manager?'

The beauty of surprise—good or bad—was that no one in the world could keep a calm face through it, however cool the person's temperament. Not even the Irish, many of whom could pass a lie detector test due to their ability to control their emotions. Jamie knew that, when genuinely surprised, an unprepared mind couldn't mask its real feelings.

'Are you looking for me?' Jamie waited for the man to turn and face him.

The man's eyes grew wide in alarm, his face turned rigid with fear, and his hands twitched in reflex.

Jamie's little surprise had scared the hell out of him.

He was the enemy. Jamie knew that the surprise had tilted the equation in his favour, but he had a window of not more than three seconds. He took a step towards the man and hit him under the chin, following that with a blow to the solar plexus. Then, as the man fell, he kicked him in the kidneys. The man fell like a tree cut with precision and was unconscious even before he hit the floor.

Jamie fished through the man's pockets and found his cell phone and a few visiting cards. He was surprised. The man was a journalist, of all the things. He couldn't help smiling. Not the police, not the intelligence service, not even the fucking Israelis. The man who lay before him was a stupid journalist. He dragged him into the adjoining toilet and wondered if he should kill him. In the end, he decided against it. Too many people dead would do more harm than good. In any case, he had just killed a man, sating his hunger to kill. What harm could a journalist do to him anyway?

After turning the door knob a few times to jam the toilet's lock, he returned to the waiting lounge. It was evening, and the chances of anyone visiting the airport manager's office were small. At least for the next ten to twelve hours.

Jamie looked around suspiciously. No one seemed even remotely interested in him. His flight to Bangkok was out of Mumbai. He'd been asked to take a circuitous route, in case the surveillance caught up with him. The boarding of his Mumbai flight was announced. He got a boarding pass and slipped inside after the security check. The plane was small, but that was no problem, as there weren't many people flying. Soon he would be on his way to Mumbai. As soon as he arrived, he planned to transfer to the international terminal and hop on a connecting flight to Dubai, then to Singapore from there. From the island nation, he would take a three-hour road trip to Kuala Lumpur to shake off the possibility of anyone tracking his air route. And finally, he would arrive in Bangkok, the city he knew so well, by late tomorrow night. He was desperately looking forward to it.

After settling into his seat in the aircraft, he took out his phone to switch it off. But at that moment, it began to buzz. It was his boss, and he picked up instantly.

'Where are you?'

'On the flight to Mumbai.'

The air hostess smiled and asked him to switch off his phone. Jamie didn't want any trouble, but he had to speak for a few seconds more. He placed his palm over the receiver and said, wearing his best smile, 'Exactly thirty seconds.'

She didn't return his smile and walked away. The doors had already been shut, and soon the plane would begin to taxi.

'Why did you kill in Udaipur?'

The question hit him hard. How in the world had his boss, who was in Tehran, learned about the killing in under two hours?

'He failed in his mission,' Jamie swallowed hard, but his mouth was already dry. The effort turned his forehead moist.

'Missions are assigned by us, not you. Your job is only to execute the missions that *we* authorize. You have been trained to work alone. One more lapse like this and...'

The call was disconnected. Jamie switched the phone off and pocketed it. The manner in which his boss had spoken to him made him wonder if he was doing the right thing by working for him. As a true soldier of Islam, he had every right to make his own decisions.

A woman was seated next to him. As the plane soared into the night sky, her feminine smell enveloped him, in the process dragging his senses in the one direction he didn't want to go—toward Sherry Bing. He shut his eyes, clenched his fists, and eventually fell asleep, aware of the weight of the small cell phone in his pocket.

Chapter 27

ACP Rao Sachin walked out of the conference room in North block at the conclusion of the emergency meeting. He had briefed the members of the National Security Council with what the police knew about the murderer and the plans of its intelligence wing to nab him. The Home minister had chaired the meeting, and the National Security Advisor to the prime minister and a few joint secretaries had attended the briefing. The ACP had been directed to employ his best men to find out who had murdered the Israeli woman.

All present voiced their concerns, one by one, while the others ate powdery Britannia Good Day biscuits and slurped tea from white china. As soon as the meeting was over, they walked away in a hurry. ACP Rao was left all by himself. He ignored the cup of tea before him. He wondered, perhaps for the hundredth time, why the only time he saw ministers and senior bureaucrats really look busy was when they moved from one venue to another down the long corridors of the North Block. Most of them, otherwise, were as useless as tits on a bull.

But they had okayed his plan in the end. He liked working in the field, and therefore, this was an opportunity to celebrate.

His phone buzzed. It was his office.

'Sir, we have tracked that number you gave us. It is moving toward the airport in Udaipur as we speak.'

'I am on my way to the Delhi airport; book me on the next flight to Udaipur. Ask our team to meet me on my arrival in Udaipur. Meanwhile, keep tracking that number. As soon as I touch down, I want an update about where this rogue journalist is. What is he hiding from us? Is he really the killer?'

He disconnected. He slid into his car and asked the driver to take him to the airport. His house was on the way, and he called his wife to pack up some things for a couple of days.

As his car moved through traffic, the ACP tried to understand the motivation behind a journalist stepping into police territory. The man was a freelance journalist, and his boss had said that he was acting independently. It was unusual for a freelance journalist to take such a big risk. It didn't add up. He was also surprised at the journalist's girlfriend, who, instead of talking some sense into him, seemed to be part of his larger plan. The ACP had therefore ordered his surveillance team to also constantly monitor her number.

When they arrived at his house, the ACP's wife came down to hand over his small overnight bag. He smiled at her. The very next day was their wedding anniversary, and they both knew he wouldn't be home this time either. In five years of marriage, he had not been home even once for their anniversary. This time, he had promised her a big treat, but once again, it was not to be.

When he reached the airport, he was just in time to check in for a flight departing in half an hour. He ran and was the last man to get on the plane, out of breath and perspiring.

ACP Rao's mind was racing. The minister had said that the Israelis suspected foul play in the killing. The initial investigation by the police hadn't revealed anything. It was only after the Israelis applied pressure that the case was transferred to the Intelligence wing. The ACP had been summoned by the Additional Commissioner of Police (Intelligence), his supervisor, just the previous morning and told about the case.

'Rao, I have handpicked you for an important case. You must be aware of the murder of the Israeli tourist?'

'Yes, sir.' His thoughts turned towards the anniversary promise he had made to his wife, but he kept his expression neutral.

'Pick your best team. There's something fishy about the woman's death. Get cracking.'

After being waved away, ACP Rao had returned to his room and spoken to the SHO in charge of Daryaganj. Though the verdict of the doctors during the autopsy was murder by suffocation, the killer had not left any evidence. ACP Rao swung into action and, with a crack team of four, got the entire hotel vacated. The owner had warned him of dire consequences, but before he could get a court order to evict them, the game would be over. Once the hotel was empty, Rao systematically searched the victim's room, her entire floor, and even the roof.

The search didn't reveal anything. There were no leads at all. He called the staff one by one to ask questions. It was when he was speaking to the night receptionist, Raju, that he smelt a rat. Years of interrogation had honed ACP Rao's ability to spot hesitation and fear in people. Raju was one glaring example.

Once he picked up on that, the rest was easy. After one slap and a few warnings, Raju sang like a canary. He told the ACP everything about that night. He said he had not seen the killer. But for now, ACP Rao was happy. He had a lead. There was someone else hot on the trail. The journalist's name was Vicks Menon. The ACP soon found out that the man was an alcoholic and had recently lost his job due to non-performance. Raju gave him Vicks' number, and ACP Rao's surveillance team tracked the phone to a hotel at Udaipur. He dispatched a team of two to Udaipur, hoping to catch the journalist before he woke up. Unfortunately, there were no available flights for the next seven hours, so he had to send them by road. By the time they arrived, Vicks had left the hotel, and this time, his phone was switched off.

The ACP never liked to use women to get information, but he was left with no choice. He was clever and managed to get the new number Vicks was using when Tonya called him to inform him about the police investigation, just as ACP Rao had hoped she would.

CHAPTER 28

ARIEL ARRIVED IN the ambassador's room and shook his extended hand. Adam Shatner stood next to the ambassador.

'Shalom.' The ambassador smiled and pointed to the sofa, rounding the table to escort the two of them to the far end of the room.

'Shalom, ambassador.'

They sat down, and after an awkward few seconds, the ambassador began. 'I was waiting for you, Mr. Miller. I've been told what you have gone through for our motherland. I'm honoured to meet you.'

'Thank you.'

'Regarding the letter you brought for that unfortunate woman, Sherry Bing—I have learned that the paper contains very sensitive information about the enemy. I don't have a precise idea of what is mentioned in it; these things, as you know, are on a need-to-know basis...' After a brief pause, he continued, 'Please call this number immediately.'

Ariel accepted the slip of paper the ambassador gave him and looked at the number.

'Thank you, but I would rather call my boss.' The ISD code was for Tel Aviv, but Ariel didn't know whose number it was.

'I am afraid you can't call your boss. This information cannot go through more people than necessary.'

Ariel heard the frustration in the ambassador's voice. If he disagreed again, the frustration would give way to anger. What the hell was in that letter? The ambassador was every bit on edge. 'Mr. Ambassador, I will do what you ask, but I need to make this call in private.' He stood up and moved to the phone.

'Of course.' The ambassador walked out of the room, Adam in tow. Ariel winked at the defence attaché as he went past him and liked the puzzlement on his face.

Ariel knew he would be watched, so he looked at the paper as he dialed his boss's number from memory. The conversation was over in less than three minutes, but it dealt Ariel a severe blow. He sat down on the sofa. The door opened moments later; just as he had expected, they were watching him. The confirmation of his intuition added a little to his confidence.

'What is it?' the ambassador asked as he settled on the edge of the sofa, almost like an anxious school child.

'Nothing that I can share with you.' Ariel hated this and expected it would provoke a reaction, but it was time to put the ambassador in his place.

'You are in India, and I am sure whatever you have been told, it should be shared with me.'

Ariel looked at him helplessly. His eyes flew to the wall behind the ambassador's chair. It was covered with military honours: medals, mementos, epaulets encased in glass boxes, and a couple of pictures of the ambassador in full military regalia. The ambassador was a retired senior officer from the Israeli Army. His behavior matched his background, and it also explained the body language of his defence attaché.

'I am sorry, Your Honour, Mr. Ambassador; you know I can't share. I'm sure you appreciate the fact that I am under the direct orders of a higher authority,' Ariel said, trying to sugarcoat his refusal. He had been categorically directed not to share what he was told with anyone.

'Very well then.' The ambassador pretended to suddenly remember something important and went over to shuffle the pile of papers on his desk. It was an indication to Ariel that their meeting was over.

Ariel returned to his room, stared at the camera for a few seconds, and lay down on the bed. His mind was busy. What he had just heard made him want to scream in anger. But the room wasn't private enough for that. Possibly the toilet was, he thought. He got up, walked inside, and searched the small room thoroughly. No camera here. They had spared this little eight by eight foot cubicle. He finally looked at himself in the mirror and released an angry cry.

Over the phone, his boss had said that the Iranians were preparing to equip their ballistic missiles with chemical warheads. The warheads were about to be shipped. The plan was to target Tel Aviv from the sea. The latitude and longitude of the factory where the warheads were manufactured and stored was mentioned in the paper. It was less than ten kilometers from where Ariel had lived in Tehran. He had passed it every day on his way to work for the last five years, thinking that it was a shoe factory.

The paper revealed another thing. His failure. It hit him hard. At one point, he had received orders from his boss to check out that particular building. It was last winter, and the information had reached him through a chain of human carriers. He had checked, but not thoroughly. The reason for his failure was his favorite prostitute. He could make a private search of the place only on Sunday evenings, and that was the time he spent with the only woman in the world who called him handsome. So he had done a half-hearted job, sent a message back that there was nothing there, and never bothered to check again.

Ariel met his own eyes in the mirror and whispered, 'I will do damage control. It's my duty now to undo my mistake.'

CHAPTER 29

ACP RAO LOOKED through the window as the aircraft touched down in Udaipur. The first thing he did was switch his cell phone on. Vicks was last reported to be moving from the city toward the airport. The ACP was desperate for a fresh update. Even if Vicks had already flown out of Udaipur, he could find him easily, as long as he kept his phone on.

The phone began to ring as soon it was switched on. It was Sub-Inspector Vikas.

'Sir, trouble. We have found Vicks. He was locked in the toilet of the airport manager's office.'

'What? Where is he now?'

'He has been taken to the hospital.'

'I will be with you in five minutes. Meet me next to the luggage carousel.'

This was disgusting. A hit and run typical in criminal cases. It had to be someone Vicks was tailing, in all probability, the killer of the Israeli tourist. ACP Rao found Sub-Inspector Vikas a few minutes later and nodded to him. They walked to one side, out of earshot of the other travelers, and Vikas filled him in.

ACP Rao's first concern was to find out who hurt Vicks. He went to the CCTV monitor room next to the airport manager's office, flashed his ID at the CISF guards staring at the monitors, and asked for the footage that covered the corridor leading to the airport manager's office.

It took him a little over half an hour. A running Vicks was seen entering the room, and after a few seconds, a tall man who kept his head down, probably aware of the camera's position, walked inside. The door was closed. Five minutes later, the man emerged again, still keeping his head down, and walked in the direction of the lounge.

But something happened just as the man was about to pass out of range of the camera. He stuck his middle finger up, all the time looking down. The gesture was for ACP Rao, as the man clearly knew that, at some point, people would be watching this tape. Not only did he do whatever he wanted to, he had the courage to show off. The gesture smacked of over-confidence; it showed that the enemy was not scared. But where was he now?

ACP Rao knew what clothes the man was wearing: jeans and a white shirt. He decided to turn his attention to the camera that covered the check-in counters. It took him another half an hour to spot the man again. He paused the recording and began to play it one frame at a time. The time of check-in was visible behind the clerk's head. ACP Rao ran to the check-in counter, and by matching the time on the check-in records, he was able to get the name of the passenger: Mr. Sam Bradman, traveling to Mumbai. Nationality: Panamanian.

ACP Rao called Mumbai, and they returned his call after fifteen minutes to say that no such person had departed from Mumbai. So either the man in jeans and a white shirt had left Mumbai on another fake passport or he was at large in Mumbai. In either case, it was a dreadful situation for ACP Rao. He punched the air in frustration and cursed loudly. People around him looked in his direction with frowns, which he tried his best to ameliorate by smiling in return.

There had to be a way. There always was. He knew it. And it came to him in a flash: Vicks, the rogue journalist. He would know more.

'Let's go the hospital,' he announced.

Before Sub-Inspector Vikas could move or acknowledge ACP Rao's order, he began heading towards the door.

'Sir, the vehicle is waiting. Let me call the driver.' With this, Vikas scampered after his boss.

CHAPTER 30

TONYA, WHISPERED VICKS. He tried to open his eyes, but his eyelids were heavy. Was he dreaming?

'Tonya,' he called, louder this time, and in response, felt a hand on his shoulder. The hand gently squeezed him. It was soothing, but the grip wasn't Tonya's. He would recognise her in an instant. Just by the touch of her hands, her smell, even her silence. Vicks tried sniffing the air. He smelt hospital. Yes, he was in a hospital; there was no mistaking it. But what was he doing there?

He heard a doctor's voice and a woman's, the one who had touched him perhaps. They were discussing the patient, his vitals, medications, the next time to review his condition, etc. Vicks tried to speak, but this time, words failed him as he felt a prick on his right arm, slightly below where the woman had touched. His lips turned heavy, and the voices around him changed, as if they were under water.

Finally, a blanket pulled him into its folds. It was dark and frightening, and he gave himself up without wanting to. Vicks was no longer in control of himself. It was others who controlled him. His final thought, before the power to think was sucked into a black hole, was of Tonya. Her smile the first time he had taken her on a date. She had looked beautiful.

CHAPTER 31

ACP RAO WALKED into Vicks' room and greeted the nurse. Sub-Inspector Vikas's partner, Inspector Ashutosh, who had accompanied Vikas from Delhi, was also present. He looked at the ACP through droopy eyes, got to his feet as a mark of respect, then sat down again. ACP Rao knew all about him. He had handpicked Ashutosh because hidden behind the sleepy demeanour were a sharp brain and a rare power of observation that didn't miss anything.

ACP Rao nodded back to him and turned his attention to the nurse. 'Sister, how is the patient now?'

'May I know who you are?'

He smiled. Though the question offended him, he took out his ID and said, 'We need to know. It is important.'

'Sir, you have to speak to the doctor first. He is across the hall in the room marked "Duty Doctor".'

'Thank you.'

Vikas stayed with the nurse watching over Vicks, and Inspector Ashutosh gave ACP Rao the details of Vicks' condition on the way to the doctor's office. Talking to the doctor was now just a formality, but one he wanted to complete.

The doctor looked every bit a doctor: ill-fitting

clothes, thick glasses, and a permanent calm on his face, as if he were in collaboration with God.

'It's a concussion. He is out of danger as far as I can tell. But I am not one hundred percent certain about the injury to his head. The neurosurgeon is on the way. We will know in an hour, okay?'

'I want to question your patient. It's something we need to do as the police. Time is running out, and the man has important information.'

'Only after the neurosurgeon clears him, sir. In any case, the patient will not wake up for at least four hours, since we sedated him a few minutes ago.'

They returned to Vicks' room, and Ashutosh sat down beside Vicks, his eyes as droopy as before. The nurse was flipping through a magazine on the other side of the patient.

After a minute, Sub-Inspector Vikas returned to the room with two cups of tea in his hands. The ACP accepted one and sat down in a chair. The nurse smiled at Vikas and said thank you before accepting the other cup. Vikas left the room to get more tea.

The police weren't exactly staring at a dead end, but ACP Rao was on edge. It was close to midnight, and in a few minutes, a new day would begin. The anticipation of his wedding anniversary added to his edginess. Here he was in a hospital, far away from home, waiting for a patient he had never met before to wake up.

Being a policeman was tough. But it was what ACP Rao Sachin had wanted to do all his life. He grew up in the small town of Rewari in the state of Haryana, and because his father was a soldier with the Indian army, he'd always wanted to become one. But the library at his school had a good collection of books by Agatha Christie and books about Sherlock Homes, and he ended up reading them in his free time. One by one, he finished them all. He liked the fact that capturing a dreaded criminal was a mind game.

He remembered that once, when his father had come home on leave from Kashmir, where he was posted at the time, a school-going Rao Sachin had asked him, 'Dad, is working for the police department as noble as working for the military?'

The senior Sachin had smiled. The ACP had a vivid recollection of that moment even now. His father said, 'Son, like the military, policemen also wear uniforms and work for national security. The only difference is that, while the people in the military protect the nation from external aggression, the police take care of internal security and maintain peace.'

Rao Sachin had been happy to hear that and decided to become a top police officer one day, preparing for it from that moment on. After graduating from Delhi University, he took the civil services exam and opted to join the Indian Police Service (IPS). At the academy, his analytical skills and resourcefulness in solving complicated crimes during the practical examinations secured him a place in the coveted intelligence branch.

But often, trouble comes from the choices people make, and his story was no different. Soon after completing his training, he realized that no one respected policemen in India. And to make matters worse, the politicians were working to convince the general public that the police service was nothing but a bunch of thieves. Instead of losing his head over it, he decided to prove them wrong. But he gave up after a few years. The work of the police, he now knew, would never be respected in India. People would throng to the ashrams of oversexed religious *babas*, queue for hours to listen to spineless politicians, and break every law of the land at the drop of a hat, and yet blame the police for the chaos. He decided, eventually, to do his best and expect nothing in return.

The ACP was brought back to the present by the arrival of a team of four officers from the Udaipur police department. Greetings were exchanged. The ACP went with them to the cafeteria to share notes and discuss the details of the case.

The Udaipur police team told him that they'd been delayed in reaching the hospital by the murder of a hotel security manager called Amar Rathore at a luxurious heritage hotel hours before. The victim was found dead in the room of a British national called Jamie, who was nowhere to be found. He was on the run. Roadblocks had been set up in all directions, and the airport, bus stops, and railway stations were being watched.

ACP Rao nodded but thought nothing of it. It had taken place on the turf of the Udaipur police and was, therefore, not his problem. His focus was on finding out what Vicks knew about Sherry Bing's murderer.

Suddenly struck by a thought, he turned to face the inspector from the Udaipur police department. 'What did you say the man's name was? The British guy?'

'Jamie.'

'Bingo.' He called his office and asked them to recheck. He was right. Jamie was the suspected killer, according to the website of the *India Now* newspaper. And Vicks, who now lay unconscious in the hospital, was freelancing for them. Suddenly, the wait for Vicks to wake up became more fascinating than watching paint dry.

CHAPTER 32

VICKS OPENED HIS eyes and found himself staring at an old man, who stood over him. The man was wearing a lab coat, and his teeth seemed too white.

Relieved, Vicks succeeded in moving his head after some effort. He felt a dull throbbing pain when he did so. 'Where am I?'

'In the hospital. But you are fine. My name is Doctor Mehra. I'm a neurosurgeon, Mr. Vicks. We have run all the routine tests on you, and everything is good. How do you feel?'

'Thanks, I am feeling okay, I think.' Vicks was able to move his head more freely now as he looked around the room. Two men in plain clothes and a nurse in a white uniform were also present in the room. All were standing. He tried to look more closely at them. The empty eyes of the men gave them away. They were the police, probably the ones who found him in that toilet.

'Great! We will discharge you in a few hours, as soon as the sedatives exit your system,' said the doctor. After a pause, he added, 'Just remember to see a doctor if, in the next few months, you feel dizzy for no apparent reason.'

The doctor departed, and the nurse followed him out.

Vicks' thoughts turned to the attack in the airport. How reckless of him, he thought. He had fucked up big time, forgotten the basics, and ignored the fact that keeping an eye in the rearview mirror was as much a part of an investigative reporter's job as looking ahead. 'Damn,' he whispered, and his frustration increased the throbbing pain in his head.

But the enemy had been more patient. Vicks remembered the voice that had come from behind him in the airport manager's office as he was foolishly looking out the window at the plane taking off. His adversary was so cool that he'd sounded almost sincere in his question. And before Vicks could recover from the surprise and protect himself, Jamie was all over him. The first one under the chin had dulled his reflexes, and after the blow in the solar plexus, he wasn't able to breathe. Finally, when he was kicked in the side, he'd lost consciousness.

But he hadn't died. The enemy had spared his life. Why? Probably so that once he woke up, he'd be forced to live with the frustration of his failure. Vicks closed his eyes again. He had no confidence left to face anyone. Not his boss, not the police. He just wanted to see Tonya. He would give up his stubbornness about being an investigative reporter. Perhaps he could study some more, as Tonya had said he should, and pick a decent white-collar job. The job of an investigative reporter had nearly gotten him killed. It was obviously not his cup of tea. He closed his eyes.

'Son, how are you?'

The voice was familiar, and yet it made him uncomfortable. He opened his eyes slowly and saw his father, who must have come into the room while Vicks' eyes were closed. Though his expression suggested concern, his eyes gave him away. There was a distinct sparkle in them, as if they were twinkling with excitement at Vicks' failure.

Vicks didn't bother to reply. He heard his father asking the others to leave the room so the two of them could have some private time. Feet shuffled out, and then all was quiet. He kept his eyes tightly shut, aware of his father's eyes on him.

'You asshole, you could have asked me, if you needed a job. Haven't I told you many times that everyone can't be a hero? You're a sissy. As useless and weak as your mother.'

The words stung. But Vicks couldn't do anything. He knew that reacting to the Additional Secretary at the Ministry of Home Affairs would land him into a lot of trouble. His father had the Home Minister and the Defence Minister on speed dial. The only thing Vicks could do now was stop the tears from slipping out. The bastard had mentioned his mother, whom he'd abused all her life, until the poor woman died. He didn't kill her, but he'd abused her physically and mentally for so many years that her death was just the end of a lifelong trauma. And now he was accusing Vicks' mother of being weak and him being weak too.

'Answer me!'

Vicks opened his eyes a crack. He wanted to get up and confront this man. He wanted him to go away. But he couldn't. The fact was he was still scared of him.

'You're lucky that I was in Udaipur for a holiday. I came as soon as I heard.'

Who could have informed him? Vicks carried nothing on his person that connected him to his father. No IDs in which his father's name was mentioned, no diaries with names and phone numbers, and no number in his cell phone either.

Vicks was aware that his father was angry. His eyes were closed, but he could hear his father's labored breathing, and he could picture his nostrils flaring. He had seen him like this many times. At that moment, his father was like a bull in a china shop. If Vicks even hinted at disagreement, his father would cause unthinkable destruction. He stayed calm, concentrating on not allowing the tears to leak out of his tightly closed eyes.

'Okay, listen to me,' his father said after a minute. 'I've found you a job. My friend owns a showroom for a leading clothing brand. Manage that for him. It will be easy. He has a daughter who's nice; get to know her, make friends with her. She is your future wife. Don't screw it up. I will wait for you in the car. The doctor will send you out in half an hour. We will drive straight to Delhi. Clear?'

This was a new challenge.

His father patted his cheek when he didn't disagree. The affectionate pat burnt his cheek for a long time after his father was gone.

CHAPTER 33

'YOU ARE FREE to leave the hospital now.'

The doctor had already explained that it was the shock that had knocked him unconscious and there were no serious injuries. Even the throbbing pain in his head was gone.

Vicks picked up his bag after the doctor had gone and turned to look at ACP Rao, who was studying him. They'd exchanged basic introductions earlier, but otherwise not spoken. There was no one else in the room.

'I have a few questions, Vicks. Tell me what happened. Everything from the time you started chasing this story. From Delhi.'

He had to be careful about what to tell and what not to. Vicks put his bag down again and sat down in the chair.

The ACP raised his hand. 'Before you start... Look, I am sorry. I tricked Tonya in order to find out your new number. No offence, please.'

'None taken.'

Vicks liked the frankness of the ACP. His body language suggested sincerity of purpose, and he seemed honest. Vicks didn't share the opinion of Indian politicians that all policemen were thieves. He had worked long enough as a crime reporter for *India*

Now to be aware that many of the men in khakis were organized, loyal, and worked hard to solve crimes.

But at the moment, he was caught in a desperate situation. If he walked out of the hospital, his father would forcibly drive him to Delhi. That would be a disaster. He was contemplating giving up the job of an investigative reporter, but not until after this case was finished. He was the prime suspect for a crime he did not commit. Even in a best case scenario if he escaped jail, he would be under a cloud of suspicion for the rest of his life. The truth that Jamie was the killer had to come out. Besides, his father had called him a sissy, and that had ignited a new spark of commitment. Vicks wasn't a coward, and he was going to prove that to his father. He decided to give only bare- bones details to the ACP.

After he was finished and before the ACP could ask any questions, Vicks asked, his voice small and innocent, 'Now I need your help, ACP.'

'Shoot, I'm all ears.' The ACP's over-eagerness made Vicks smile.

'My father has set a trap for me outside the hospital, and let me assure you that he is a bastard. Please rescue me.'

'Your father?'

"Yes, his name is Rajkumar Menon, and he is at present the Additional Secretary in the Home Ministry.'

'Oh, okay. That guy...' The two of them left the room and were quiet for a few seconds before the ACP spoke again, 'Yes, sure, I would love to do that.' And then, after a pause, 'I've met your father in North Block many times, and I agree with your assessment of him.'

They laughed. ACP Rao escorted him to the other end of the hospital, and they exited through the door meant for the emergency care patients. When they walked out of the hospital building, it was early morning and the trees were dripping with dew. Vicks looked up at the sky and saw an airplane high up, a jet trail behind it. And for a moment, he wondered where Jamie was.

As if in answer to his question, ACP Rao commented, 'Jamie could be anywhere by now. He used a fake identity on his flight from Udaipur to Mumbai. From there, we have no trace. Perhaps he changed his identity again. Maybe even changed his appearance. There's no way we can determine where he might be at this time.'

'I don't know what route he'll take, but I know where he's headed.'

ACP Rao stopped and looked at him. 'You are indeed smart, my friend. You should be in the police.'

'Trust me, ACP Rao sahib, the job of an investigative reporter is just like that of the police. Maybe tougher, because we are minus the guns.'

'Okay, where do you want to go now?'

'When is the next flight to Delhi?'

'In two hours.'

'I'm off to Delhi. If my father calls, please tell him that I'm still in Udaipur, investigating Amar Rathore's murder. Let him go around in circles for a while.'

'I'll certainly do that, but can I ask you something in return?'

'Shoot, I'm all ears,' Vicks said, imitating the ACP.

The ACP smiled. 'You've got to tell me where Jamie is headed.'

There was a pause for a few seconds, as they looked into each other's eyes, before Vicks whispered just one word: 'Bangkok.'

'Will you promise me that you will call me if you get into trouble?'

'What makes you think I'm going to Bangkok?'

'I am a cop, remember? I can read people's minds.'

'I will be in touch. Thanks a lot.' Vicks got into an auto-rickshaw and ordered the driver to take him to the airport. As soon as the vehicle started to move, his phone buzzed. It was Tonya.

'Vicks where the hell have you been? I've been calling you since last night. Are you all right?'

'I'm fine. Everything is okay. I was just resting.'

'No, you were not. It's in your voice. Tell me the truth; where were you?'

He didn't have the heart to lie to Tonya. If he told any more lies, she would know. 'I was in the hospital. I slipped and hurt myself. Nothing major, just a few scratches, but the stupid doctors sedated me and I couldn't hear you calling.'

'Doctors are not stupid. I was so worried... I didn't know what to do. So I called your dad.'

Vicks didn't realize how angry he was until he blurted, 'You stupid fool, why did you call him? You know how much I hate him.' There was silence, and Vicks realized his mistake. He heard her crying softly on the other end of the line.

Between sobs, she said, 'I was so worried... If something happened to you... Your father was the only one I knew who'd have influence... you know, with the police and all.'

Her concern began to cut through his anger, and soon, he was feeling annoyed with himself. In her shoes, he would have done something equally drastic. After exchanging a few more sentences, Vicks said, 'I will be arriving in Delhi in three hours.'

'I will be waiting at the airport.'

'No, please don't do that. I will come and meet you at the hospital.'

'Do you know where I am at this moment?'

'No.' Vicks was amused. How he could know?

'I'm at the Delhi airport with a ticket to Udaipur in my hand. When no one could tell me where you were, I decided to find out on my own. I will cancel this ticket and wait for you here.'

Vicks was moved, and the prospect of being with her again electrified him from the inside, 'I love you, Tonya.'

'I love you too.'

When the auto rickshaw arrived at the airport, he got out, tipped the driver with a hundred rupee note, and smiled like a writer who'd just been told that he won a major contest.

CHAPTER 34

WHILE VICKS WAS on his way to Delhi, eagerly anticipating being with Tonya—who had, after so many weeks, finally acknowledged being in love with him—the communication lines between Israel, India, and Iran were burning like never before. An officer on special duty, who was actually a hacker at the NIA's nerve center at RK Puram in New Delhi, had become suspicious at the increased traffic and flagged some of the locations. He shared the information with the officers of the National Security Council and was directed to monitor it more closely.

Two additional hackers joined his team of about a dozen cyber experts, and they began to concentrate on the emergence of a pattern. The nerve center of their operations was actually a private company contracted secretly by the Indian government to monitor geographical areas within certain countries that they had reason to believe contained rogue elements sponsored by the state or extremist groups. Besides phones and faxes, they monitored email accounts and the social media postings from certain ISPs.

***

Upon arrival at the Delhi airport, Vicks saw Tonya waving at him from the visitor's lounge. He waved back and ran towards her, his only baggage, his shoulder bag, strapped on his back. They hugged, and Vicks tried to smother Tonya's sobs by tightening his arms around her. The two of them stayed like that until the lumps in their throats subsided and their breathing normalized.

After they finally let go, Vicks and Tonya walked hand in hand out of the airport and hired a taxi to go home. She leaned her head against his shoulder as the city zipped past. Each turn that the driver negotiated and each time he slowed to drive over a bump gave Vicks an excuse to edge closer to her. By the time, they arrived, Tonya was asleep. It was probably the relief, he thought. He didn't want to disturb her, but they had to get out of the taxi.

He gently shook Tonya, and she opened her eyes. They were wide with alarm at first, but calm descended on her as soon as she saw him. After paying the driver, they walked into Vicks' house. Tonya was carrying an overnight bag, and it gave Vicks hope of convincing her to stay with him. This time, he would make no mistakes.

She walked into the small living room and sat down in the sofa chair. As he took the other sofa chair, stillness enveloped the two of them.

As the seconds slipped by without a conversation starting, Vicks was overcome by a caveman lust. His body wanted to make love to her right now, but he knew it was not the right thing to do. He decided to keep his desires in check and instead asked if she wanted coffee.

An hour later, after they had finished their coffee and Vicks had updated her on the progress of the case, a call from his boss interrupted Vicks' further hopes of being close to Tonya.

'I heard about you being hit, man. That was bad. Anyway, where are you now and what's next?'

Vicks was angry at the businesslike approach, as if he had soiled his shirt accidently during a tea party. Nothing more. But he restrained himself. 'I am on it.'

His boss laughed. 'On it? Where, in Delhi? Don't fool yourself, Vicks. It was for precisely this reason that I fired you. You're good, but you overestimate yourself.'

Vicks' anger rose further. 'I am on it means I am *on it.* If you want more information, I need more money. I have to get to Bangkok.'

'Whoa, whoa, man... Take it easy, Mr. Firebrand Investigative Journalist. How much?'

'Two lakhs.' In his peripheral vision, Vicks saw Tonya's expression change. She did not like this conversation one bit.

'I will transfer only one lakh as I'd transferred one lakh earlier today after your last call. Now get on with it, and get me something worthwhile.'

Vicks heard a click. His boss had had the last word. But Vicks now had the money.

Tonya had walked out onto the balcony, and he joined her there. She was staring at the trees, her eyes empty, not really looking at anything in particular. Tears streamed down her face.

'I am sorry. But I need to do this.' Vicks stammered through the sentence.

'What about us? Why are you messing with me?' Tonya was furious now, glaring at him.

Vicks felt small and selfish. His eyes dropped, unable to meet Tonya's. He knew she was right. Going ahead with the investigation gave her the message that his job was more important to him than she was. That he didn't care. Yet, he knew that wasn't the case. He thought of telling her about his father's visit to the hospital and how he'd called Vicks a sissy. *I'm not a sissy*, he wanted to shout at the top of his voice, but words failed him. He was confused and frustrated. Even in this mess, one thing was clear: he would prove his father wrong. He owed that much to his mother.

Vicks chose his words carefully, 'Look, I need you to hear me out.'

Tonya turned away, crying inconsolably now. Vicks put his hand on her shoulder, but she shook it off and walked inside the house.

He waited on the balcony for five minutes, giving her time to compose herself. If he spoke now, it would further agitate her. If there was one thing Vicks didn't want Tonya to feel, it was sadness.

When Vicks came back into the living room finally, Tonya was gone. He checked the other rooms, but there was no sign of her. He noticed that her bag was missing too and ran down the stairs to the road. It was deserted, except for the few cars parked at the curb. Tonya had once again abandoned him.

Chapter 35

With a determined look on his face, Ariel was driven out through the gates of the Israeli embassy in New Delhi in a van. Earlier, he had spent an hour with the defence attaché, to work out a strategy.

At the heart of the conundrum was the fact that there was a killer on the loose. Someone had murdered an Israeli citizen vacationing in India because she was waiting to meet Ariel in a nondescript hotel. The police had stated that the killer was in Rajasthan, and a local newspaper had updated its website a few hours ago with the name and picture of someone called Jamie who it identified as the murderer. The paper further added that the killer was hiding in Udaipur.

The police obviously knew more than what they'd shared. It was their standard operating procedure. They liked to play guessing games with criminals, going public with only a few details and stressing that their information was limited so the criminals could never be sure how much they knew. That left them so on edge that they made mistakes, which on many occasions simplified the work of the police.

The newspaper owners, however, were even more crooked. For them, sharing information was a business, and they leaked it slowly to make sure that people remained hooked on their stories and they made their money through subscriptions and advertisements. For the newspapers, it was the money, but for the police, it was their ego. If criminals were dangerous, Ariel thought, the police were even more dangerous, just criminals in uniform. They were two sides of the same coin.

From the embassy, Ariel headed straight to the police commissioner's office. The meeting had been difficult to arrange, Adam had said, but he was able to somehow convince the commissioner to meet with Ariel for five minutes. The topic was Sherry Bing's murder, and Ariel's cover was that he had arrived from Tel Aviv to watch events unfold as the case progressed. He was representing the intelligence service of his country but would remain solely an observer. Since nobody in India knew who Ariel was, he could easily pass himself off as someone who had just landed.

When Ariel arrived, the commissioner received him with a smile and shook his hand enthusiastically. It was a typical Indian welcome, and Ariel tried to reciprocate with equal fervor before gently brushing his fingers against the suit that he had bought the previous evening with the embassy's money. There were three chairs, and Ariel took the one in the middle so he was sitting directly across from the commissioner.

'Mr. Commissioner, I bring you the compliments of the government of Israel.'

'Thank you. Do wish the same on my behalf to the ambassador, and through him your government. Now tell me, what can I do for you?' The commissioner looked at him over the top of his half-moon reading glasses.

'I am here for an update on the Sherry Bing case.'

The commissioner seemed a shade frustrated, and when he spoke, Ariel realized the reason. 'I have already shared every detail that we know with your embassy.'

'Yes, sir. But it is not enough. I think you need to commit more resources. She was an Israeli citizen, and my government has sent me all the way from Tel Aviv to see that the Indian agencies don't leave any stone unturned.'

'I am doing everything that is necessary. The best people are on the job. We have a review meeting scheduled later today, and I will remember your point and bring it up before the committee.'

Ariel smiled. The meeting was progressing exactly as he had hoped. He had nothing more to discuss.

The commissioner went on: 'I have learned that you are from the Israeli Secret Service. We have great admiration for your organization, but please be warned... don't poke your nose into our business while you are here in India. I hope you understand me clearly.'

'Crystal.' Ariel found the manners of the commissioner a little offensive, but had it been the other way around, he knew the Israelis would have dealt with an Indian taking too much interest in much the same way.

'Now, I wish I could offer you tea, but I am very busy at the moment.'

'No need, Mr. Commissioner. I appreciate your time.' Ariel got to his feet and walked out, after exchanging another Indian handshake with the man.

CHAPTER 36

ON A BACK road about two kilometers from the police commissioner's office, work had begun as soon as Ariel arrived from the embassy. The vehicle was disguised as a television van that had broken down, and two men were pretending to repair it, tools scattered on the side of the road.

After his meeting with the commissioner was over, Ariel walked the distance to the van and got into the back. Inside, Adam gave him a thumbs-up in greeting. It meant that Ariel had correctly placed a transmitter under the table in the police commissioner's office. The small transmitter, not more than one inch in diameter, was fitted with a battery that could last for seventy-two hours. It had an adhesive on one side that could stick to any surface.

As Ariel settled in the van, he heard the commissioner talking on the phone. It had something to do with security preparations at a local stadium where a holy man was scheduled to fast indefinitely.

'These Indians,' Adam said. 'They think every problem can be solved by fasting. It's in their blood. Even their religion teaches them to starve.'

Ariel didn't respond. It was a hint for Adam to shut up. They listened to the conversation, which was partly in Hindi. There were two more men in the van, turning the dials from time to time to squelch the static in the VHF transmission. One of them was a Hindi-to-Hebrew translator, and since he didn't say anything, Ariel imagined that the discussion wasn't relevant.

The day outside was cold but bright. This was stage two of the operation. Stage one had been the planting of the bug. Stage three would commence once they had what they were looking for and Ariel went in again to recover the bug. It would be tricky, he thought.

After the phone conversation, there was dead silence for about ten minutes. And then suddenly, there were voices in the room. Someone was visiting. The operator killed the squelch and raised the volume. The police knew phones could be tapped and, therefore, didn't use them anymore to communicate confidential matters. But when people met behind closed doors, secrets were discussed.

Someone started to speak: 'Sir, the killer flew out of Udaipur last night. He attacked a journalist who was apparently tailing him. Before that, he murdered a hotel security manager.'

'Where has he gone?'

'Disappeared. We are doing all we can, but he is obviously not a novice. If he changes his appearance often and uses multiple passports, we could lose him.'

'Hmm...' There was a pause. 'The Israelis are getting restless. Please be careful.'

'Yes, sir.'

'So what have you planned now, Rao?'

Adam smiled, about to show his pleasure at the discovery of the name of the officer in charge of this case, but as soon as his eyes met Ariel's, which were expressionless, he stopped.

'Sir, I need to go to Bangkok. That's where our killer might be going, according to the journalist, Vicks Menon. In the absence of any other leads, there is no harm in going along with his hunch. Another thing, sir; I met Vicks in Udaipur. He seems to be a nice guy but slightly naïve. If Delhi police are in Bangkok, we might be able to save him if he does something disastrous.'

'But why would a journalist take such a risk?'

'Survival, sir. Plain and simple. He lost his job to a rival, and now he wants to go all out to get it back.'

'Good, keep me posted.'

The room was quiet for a few minutes. When the men in the van heard the commissioner talking to someone over the phone again, they realized that the meeting had been adjourned.

Ariel nodded to the operators. They had everything they needed. It was time to launch stage three.

He went back into the building and was escorted to the commissioner's office once more. The security staff had seen him earlier, and when he said the commissioner had called him back in, they let him in. Once he reached the commissioner's secretary, Ariel smiled and said, 'I'm sorry to bother you, miss, but I left my pen in the other room by mistake.'

The secretary hesitated, smiled, and asked him

to wait. She got up from her chair and went into the commissioner's office. This was a disaster. There was no pen. She emerged from the room moments later and said, 'Sir, there's no pen inside. You must have dropped it somewhere else.'

'No, I checked the route I took out of the building. Couldn't find it. Can I go inside and check myself?'

The secretary hesitated again, picked up the phone, and spoke to the commissioner over the intercom. Then she turned and told him he could go in.

Ariel was relieved to see the commissioner still talking on the phone. He had secretly hoped for that. It meant that his powers of observation were compromised at the moment. Ariel bent down, removed the transmitter, and straightened. The commissioner was looking at him with a question in his eyes.

'I forgot this, sir.' He extended his hand to show him a black pen he was holding. With the other, he dropped the transmitter into his coat pocket.

The commissioner put the phone down and took the pen. He turned it around and opened it, a worried expression on his face that Ariel knew would be temporary. After satisfying himself, he handed it back to Ariel. 'Sorry, I had to check,' the commissioner said, meaning the apology.

'No sir, I am sorry. The pen has sentimental value; otherwise, I wouldn't have bothered you again.'

Ariel walked out, bowed to the secretary, and exited the building. He climbed into the van, and they drove back to the embassy, the mission a success.

Back in the commissioner's office, the secretary walked in with a puzzled look on her face. 'Sir, I checked thoroughly. There was no pen.'

'Are you sure?'

'One hundred percent.'

'Okay, we have this man's picture on our security cameras. Pass it on to ACP Rao and ask him to station two boys outside the Israeli embassy. Keep this man under surveillance.'

'I don't think he's left the building yet. Do you want me to inform the security staff to stop him so that we can check him thoroughly?'

The commissioner thought about it for a while but decided against it in the end. Foreigners caused too much trouble. The government would come down heavily on him, and at the moment, he had his hands full. 'No, but thank you.'

She left, the puzzled look still on her face.

CHAPTER 37

TONYA HAD LEFT Vicks once again. He felt nailed to the floor, surrounded by questions.

Why hadn't Tonya given him a chance to explain?

Should he just forget the enemy who'd almost killed him?

Should he say yes to his father and become a dull salesman? Accept that he was a sissy?

The more he thought, the more the pain in his head resurfaced. The doctor had said there were no internal injuries, so why this pain? He sat down, holding his head with both hands. This loneliness was killing him. He could smell Tonya everywhere in the house, but she wasn't there. There was no one in the world Vicks could confide his fears to. He had no way of knowing if what he had decided to do was the right thing or not.

His father's words still echoed in his mind. He had called him a coward.

He thought about his mother, and the pain in his head multiplied. His father had abused her. And in the end, she'd died without telling the world what she had gone through. Vicks had cried his heart out the day she passed away, but his father had been indifferent. At the funeral, he'd even scolded Vicks, hissing through clenched teeth that men didn't cry.

Bastard.

Vicks opened the cupboard and gulped rum straight from the bottle of Old Monk. He wasn't himself anymore and had no idea what he was doing. The alcohol made him dizzy, and he sat down on the kitchen floor. He wasn't crying. He felt a strange anger at all those around him. Even Tonya.

Night fell outside. The phone rang a few times. But by then, Vicks had given in greedily to the numbness that the alcohol brought. He slept right there, on the kitchen floor, floating away from his fears and frustrations.

When Vicks woke, it was still dark. Groggy, he sat up and wondered what time it was. Just then, he noticed there was someone seated beside him. And then the smell reached him. He got to his feet and switched on the light. Staring at him, her back resting against the wall in the kitchen, was Tonya. Her eyes were unblinking, and her cheeks were wet with tears.

'I am sorry, Vicks.'

He looked at the half-empty Old Monk rum bottle next to where he had slept and hung his head. He had broken his promise. 'I am sorry, Tonya.'

She got up and extended her arms towards him, and Vicks pulled her close. There was a hint of dawn breaking outside. Vicks felt her softness melt against his body. He smelt her hair, brushed his lips over her cheeks, and found her trembling lips. Passion ignited in a flash, and the two of them left the kitchen for the bedroom.

Later, when they lay side by side on the bed, Tonya was the first to speak. 'Promise me that you will be more careful this time.'

He turned to look at her. She wasn't crying. There was a firmness in her voice that he saw mirrored in her eyes. 'I will be careful, I promise.'

Vicks pushed the blanket aside and went into the kitchen, where he switched on his laptop. While it started up, he went out and stood on the balcony, watching the birds on the trees outside. After some time, he felt Tonya's fingers slip into his and give a tug. They walked to the dining table adjacent to the kitchen, where Tonya had already prepared and placed two cups of tea.

'When will you leave?' she asked after they had finished their tea.

'Very soon.'

This case had tested everything to its limits: Vicks' journalistic abilities, his relationship with Tonya, his alcohol addiction, and finally his tortuous relationship with his father. And yet, he felt determined to win.

'I'd better get ready,' Tonya said. 'My consultation hours at the hospital start at ten.'

Vicks watched her go to the bathroom and turned his attention to his laptop. *India Now* had transferred the money into his bank account. Satisfied, he booked a seat on the next flight out of Delhi. He would have to leave in an hour, and Tonya would have enough time to see him off before going to the hospital to see her patients. He desperately needed the comfort of her presence until the very last minute.

When they reached the T3 terminal of the Indira Gandhi International Airport, Vicks hugged Tonya and repeated his promise. 'I will be careful. I am just a journalist chasing a good story.'

She nodded, and Vicks saw that a lump in her throat was choking off her words. He waited, and after a few seconds, she succeeding in overcoming it. 'I love you.'

'I love you too.'

Vicks kissed her and walked into the terminal. He paused once to turn, and she was right there, in the same spot he'd left her. He waved, and she waved back. Then he turned abruptly and walked deep into the airport, away from the woman he loved and into the waiting arms of danger.

He had nothing to go on, except a picture and the name Jamie, which the killer was probably not using anymore. It would be like finding a needle in a haystack. But that was precisely his job, to find needles in haystacks, and he'd done it many times before. Hints came from unexpected quarters. This time too, he hoped, things would work out for the best.

Perhaps he could begin with the areas frequented by criminals. A man like Jamie—who was a ruthless killer, having killed his girlfriend, with whom everyone thought he was in love—would definitely have friends in the criminal world. The picture Vicks was carrying would cause a surprise or two, and once he caught Jamie's scent, the game would start.

Behind Vicks at the check-in counter of the Thai airways flight, a man he didn't know queued up. The man had a forgettable face but for his nose, which was exceptionally long. After Vicks got his boarding pass and moved away, the man with the long nose came up and smiled at the pretty girl across the counter.

She inspected his tickets, tapped a few keys on the computer, and smiled as she handed him his boarding pass, 'Have a pleasant flight, Mr. Miller.'

The man didn't acknowledge her pleasantry. He left the counter and began to follow Vicks, a gentle smile on his lips.

CHAPTER 38

ACP Rao and the police commissioner paused their discussion when the door opened and a man with binoculars dangling around his neck came into the room. He was a police constable in a crisp uniform, a big smile on his lips. After a smart salute, he announced, 'Sir, the van is gone.'

He turned and walked out before either of them could respond.

'What is this, Rao?'

'Sir, when you called me this morning and told me about the meeting the Israeli embassy was pressing so hard for, I smelt a rat.'

The commissioner gestured for him to hurry up with the reason, his expression still confounded.

'I knew they were up to something. The man who came to meet you came in a van. They pretended that the van had broken down while he came in to meet you. And no sooner had I met with you and told you what they wanted to hear he came back inside.'

'But how could they hear what we talked about? If you know about the pen he came back for, let me assure you that there was nothing in it. I checked it myself.'

'Sir, the pen had nothing to do with it. Somehow, he planted a bug when he was here the first time, and he came to recover it under the guise of getting back the pen, which was never in the room, as your secretary told you.'

'You spoke with her too.'

'Yes, sir. I had to know more. I thought that, before I brought the matter to you, I should check all the angles.'

The commissioner pushed back his chair and smiled. 'I get the picture. But the question is: how did he plant the bug?'

ACP Rao was already on his knees and feeling under the commissioner's big mahogany table. He pulled his fingers out after they came across a sticky spot and told the commissioner what he'd found.

'Okay Rao, but if you knew about the bug all along, why did you divulge all those details during our meeting?'

'Sir, I was playing them. I gave them information because I want them to find out why that woman was killed. I am sure they know more than they're sharing with us. The NIA has picked up some unusually frequent communications along some lines they're watching. There is definitely more to the killing.'

'But if we want them to find the killer as well, why not make them collaborators and tell them everything upfront?'

'Sir, the plan is to make them stick their necks out. We need to figure out their motives in order to unravel the truth. As collaborators, they would take everything from us but give nothing in return.'

'I hope you are right on this, ACP.'

'There are no rights or wrongs in this game, sir; you know that. I will do my best. I'll be off to Bangkok soon and will keep you posted.'

ACP Rao returned home, where his wife waited for him. Since he was gone the previous day, the real date of their anniversary, they had decided to celebrate it a day later.

After they had cut the cake and enjoyed a good meal that his wife had prepared at home, he dropped the next bombshell, 'I will have to go to Bangkok.'

'When?'

'Now.'

She didn't say anything, but ACP Rao felt a sudden lack of energy around them. He looked up at her and saw her struggle to smile and make it look normal. Then she said, 'And now you are going to tell me that things will improve once you are back?'

He nodded but knew in the core of his heart that there was no chance of that as long as he worked for the police. He wanted to tell her the truth but couldn't. Her sarcasm bit him, but all he did was smile in return.

CHAPTER 39

JAMIE ARRIVED IN Bangkok in a hired car. He was moody when he got out under the portico of the Mandarin Oriental Hotel. It was a luxury hotel, which came with more privacy. Not that he had anything to fear, but as a spy, he knew that after a hard patch, it was a good idea to be careful. Once the delicate period—a week or ten days—was over, he would be as good as new, a tourist looking for some fun. And at that time, he could truly move about unrestricted.

The Mandarin Oriental was a great hotel that could be accessed either by the road or by boat, as it had a small pier on its property. The views of the Chao Phraya River were great, and in the past, the hotel had played host to a number of intellectuals, writers, film stars, politicians, and other prominent figures.

Jamie liked the room that was reserved for him. It overlooked the river and was as calm as he desired.

'Do you need anything else, Mr. Alfonso?' the hotel staff member who'd escorted him to the room asked, her head bent, eyes on his chest. Well-trained, he thought with satisfaction; she would never look him in the eye.

'No, thank you.'

After his long trip, he was tired. It was still early in the morning, but he decided to take a few hours to nap and re-energize. In any case, he had no plans to sleep during the night. No sensible person looking for mind-blowing sexual experiences slept their nights in Bangkok away.

At noon, showered and wearing his best casuals, Jamie walked into the hotel's bar and took a stool. A few people chatted around him, but all the other stools at the counter were unoccupied.

The barman greeted him, and he ordered a double martini.

On his way to Bangkok from Kuala Lumpur, he had called his boss just once, using the new phone. Jamie wanted the Iranian intelligence service in Tehran to keep an eye out for the journalist, Vicks Menon. He shared the name and all the other details listed on the card he had removed from Vicks' pocket after neutralizing him at the Udaipur airport. His boss agreed and said they would set their technical snoops on the journalist. If Vicks moved even an inch, they would know.

Jamie sipped his drink and contemplated whether he'd done the right thing by not killing him.

'Another one?' the bartender asked.

'Of course.' Jamie smiled as he felt the alcohol kick his butt—a kick he desperately needed.

By three in the afternoon, a sozzled Jamie was at the Sunsilk bar a few kilometers from the hotel, a topless call girl on either side of him. Their giggles relaxed him as he bought them a round of drinks.

The music was thumping in his groin, and he felt hot in all the right places. But he wanted to extend the pleasure, wanted to tease the man in him. He drank more martinis.

Suzy, the male-to-female transgender manager of the Sunsilk bar, came to him and whispered in his ear. It was time. He followed her up the narrow flight of stairs to a ten by ten room on the third floor. There was maroon velvet everywhere, on the walls, on the floor, even on the ceiling. A chair with a low back and no arms stood in the middle of the room. The music was soft and sensuous. Suzy left him there, and he walked to the chair. There was no one else in the room. The anticipation and the alcohol heightened his senses.

He sat down in the chair as he heard Suzy leave, closing the door behind her. The lights dimmed slowly, stopping when they were just bright enough to make out the edges of the room. He was a man of the dark and was, therefore, wild with excitement. The door opened, and a figure on very high heels walked in. She began to dance slowly, removing her clothes until she had nothing on except the heels. Then she began closing in on him, like a shark approaching its prey, moving around the chair. He was ecstatic.

The first touch was a caress that lasted for only a second, sending an electric impulse through him. He liked the jab of pain the impulse brought. His pleasure increased another notch. Slowly, she began to undress Jamie. When all that remained were his boxer shorts, she started to slide her body against his skin.

The music slowed down, and so did his mind. The throbbing multiplied as she whispered words into his ears. He didn't understand their meaning, and it didn't matter. What mattered was the huskiness of her voice, the eagerness to please him oozing from it. He met her eyes and saw her wink teasingly.

'What's your name, honey?'

In response, she moved behind him and began to kiss his back as water jets started to hit them from all sides. The music became louder, and he felt like a wild animal in heat. Finally, as he began to thrust in his seat and the chair began to rock, she jumped up and sat on his lap, facing him. He smelt all of her now, heard her whisper in his ears, her thighs sliding over his groin.

Just before he exploded, she whispered, 'My name is Sherry. I am Sherry, your love.'

The name burst a dam somewhere inside Jamie, and he exploded like never before. And then it was all over. She got up and was about to leave the room when Jamie caught her hand. She tried to pull away.

The lap dancer said something in Thai, but he couldn't understand her. The door suddenly opened and bouncers appeared beside the transgender manager. They stepped forward but stopped when Jamie let her go.

He was escorted out, and by the time he got back to his hotel room, he knew that there was no point in missing Sherry. There were so many Sherrys out there. He would soon find a good one and start calling her Sherry Bing.

For the final course of his pleasure trip, Jamie ordered the most expensive lobster and some caviar from room service and drank more martinis until he fell asleep.

CHAPTER 40

VICKS GOT OFF the plane in Bangkok's Suvarnabhumi airport and stretched himself. It was his third visit to the Thai capital. Before boarding the plane in New Delhi, he had booked a hotel on the internet. As he headed straight to his hotel from the airport, another taxi began to tail his.

Thirty minutes later, when Vicks got out of his taxi, the taxi that was following him slowed down and stopped at a safe distance. The hotel was a basic B&B arrangement, which gave Ariel, the man in the waiting taxi, the impression that, like most journalists, Vicks was on a tight budget.

After checking in, Vicks picked up his small bag and walked to the lift on his own, soon reaching his room on the fifth floor. The room had a double bed and a small bathroom. There was no desk and not enough space to pace if one wanted to think. He could either sit in the chair or lie on the bed. A TV hung from the wall, facing the queen-size bed. He checked the bathroom and thought it was smaller than most closets. But it would do. Vicks was worried about his expenditures, as his boss would not give him more money unless things worked out to his liking, and the odds were really stacked against Vicks at the moment.

Bangkok was warm, which Vicks was prepared for. He quickly changed into Bermuda shorts and a round-neck tee. Pocketing his wallet and locking away his passport, he took the lift back to the lobby. Glancing both ways on the road outside the hotel, he began walking down the sidewalk. Vicks had no idea where he was headed. He had no plan. He only wanted to breathe in the city and think.

About a hundred meters down the road, there was an open-air café. Accustomed to the winter of Delhi, Bangkok felt too hot to Vicks. But he knew that his body would adjust within a few hours. Wiping the perspiration from his forehead with the back of his hand, he ordered a coffee.

The foamy beverage woke his mind to the challenge facing him. The first question was where to start. Was Jamie really in Bangkok? But Vicks knew dying men never lied, and he had seen the word 'Bangkok' written in blood right next to Amar's body. Jamie was certainly here, but it was impossible to point to a specific direction.

One good place to start, Vicks knew, were the areas where criminals usually hung out. Since Jamie was a criminal, he would feel more at home in such places. Second, Vicks had observed that Jamie had lots of money. He had lived in expensive hotels in India, eaten at fancy restaurants, and consumed pricey scotch. He also wore well-cut suits and expensive watches. The photograph was proof enough of that. So if he was indeed here, he would be in a luxury hotel. And he wouldn't feel the need to hide for two reasons, Vicks mused. One, his crimes were committed in another country, and two, he had taken every precaution to ensure no one learned what his next destination was.

Vicks paid for the coffee and resumed his aimless walk. He needed a phone. In Bangkok, unlike India, one could buy a SIM card off the shelf. He bought one, inserted it into his phone, and the first call he made was to Tonya. He wanted to tell her the name of the hotel he was staying in, but a sudden hunch stopped him before he could. Someone could be monitoring her number. Though he had told the ACP that Jamie was heading to Bangkok, he didn't want anyone to know the precise location of his hotel.

'Hi, Tonya, I have arrived, and all is well... Yes, yes, I will be careful... I love you too.'

Finding an internet café took some time, but when he did, he logged in and began searching for all the luxury hotels in Bangkok. Finally, he settled for the top three: The Peninsula, the Mandarin Oriental, and The Siam.

Vicks decided to begin with The Peninsula. But he had to be properly attired if he wanted access to the bars in these hotels. After changing into the formal trousers, long-sleeved shirt, and brogues he'd brought with him, he arrived at the hotel in a tuk-tuk. The façade of the hotel rose against the blue sky like a giant W, and Vicks was taken in by the monumental opulence of it.

The tricky part was how to ask the staff about

Jamie. If he tried to bribe them, like in Udaipur, and someone reported it, he could land in jail. He walked in and followed the signs to the River Bar. The bar had low, comfortable seating and was right beside the Chao Phraya River, offering open space and views of tourist-laden ferries cutting across brown waters. Vicks tried his best smile and asked the bartender what their finest on offer was.

'Thaijito, our signature cocktail.'

Vicks widened his smile some more and asked the bartender to bring him one. Bartenders—much like sommeliers, Vicks had noticed—were proud people, and they cared about what they served. Patrons who took their advice about drinks seriously impressed them so much that they would do anything to make their visit special. It wasn't difficult for Vicks to guess that the Thaijito would be the local answer to the Cuban mojito, but instead of White rum, it would have Thai rum. The rest of the ingredients—sugar, lime juice, soda, and mint—would be the same.

In any case, the fact that he was drinking rum brightened his mood. Was he doing the right thing by drinking alcohol again? He was only following the call of duty. Had the bartender not told him about the Thaijito, Vicks would have asked for a soft drink. The absurdity of the internal conflict made him smile.

The bartender came back and waited for Vicks to sip the fizzy cocktail from the tapered glass. Vicks looked up and showed him his best smile again, 'This thing is even better than a mojito, I swear.'

It wasn't entirely a lie. The taste was good. The soda played on the back of his tongue as racy bubbles flavoured with mint filled his nose with an aroma that suggested calm. The alcohol warmed his heart. Vicks missed Tonya. He made a mental note to bring her to this very place someday and share a Thaijito, drinking with two straws from the same glass.

It was the bartender's turn to smile. His reaction wasn't businesslike; there was a personal touch. Vicks had scored a point. He decided to add another one.

To invest further in the relationship, Vicks read his nametag and asked, 'How long have you been working here, Boon-Mee?'

'Five years.'

'Good and thanks for this.' Vicks raised his hand and Boon-Mee walked away, looking very happy.

CHAPTER 41

JAMIE WOKE UP with a start. It wasn't a bad dream; his cell phone was ringing. Only his boss knew the new number.

He searched for the phone in the darkness, and his hand fell on something that felt like another person. He jumped out of the bed, lost his balance as his leg got caught in the blanket, and fell to the carpeted floor.

The lights turned on, and his eyes flew to the woman in his bed. He was surprised. How had a woman he'd never seen before made it into his bed? He got up and pulled her out of the bed by her hand. She was naked, her eyes rounded, showing her fear. She opened her mouth to scream.

It must have been his expression. He put her down and pressed his palm over her mouth. Though the rooms were soundproof, a hysterical scream, he was sure, would seep outside to the corridor.

Jamie felt the woman struggle in his grip as he tried to tone down his anger. If he calmed down, his expression would change too, and the woman could be asked to go away quietly. After a few minutes, the woman went limp. Was she dead? Jamie looked down at her. He hadn't realized that his palm was covering not just her mouth but her nose as well.

He pushed her down on the carpet and began to give her mouth-to-mouth. After a few attempts, the girl drew in a long breath and sat up.

Jamie looked at her closely and remembered the lap dance last night. The room had been dark, but he had seen enough of her. Was this the same dancer? Had she secretly entered his room? But why would someone sneak into his room and sleep next to him in the bed?

The woman was now too scared to say or do anything. She knew that if she tried to scream, she would probably die. She sat there like a stone, looking at the floor, not meeting his eyes. Her lips moved ever so slightly, and Jamie knew she was praying.

'Name?'

'Bun Ma.' Only her lips moved.

It was a relief. Her name was not Sherry. So she was definitely not the girl who'd pleasured him during the lap dance.

She was still naked, perhaps waiting to see what he would do. She couldn't make the first move for fear that he would be angry. Or that is what Jamie thought. He fondled her breasts, loving to see them bounce. He felt the softness of her skin under his palms and smiled. Then he carried her to the bed and had sex with her. Her scared expression made him go on and on, and when he finally exploded, he collapsed on top of her. It was a very satisfying start to the day.

After a few minutes, he climbed out of the bed, gave her money, and pointed to the door. As he sat watching her, she picked up her clothes in an extreme hurry and vanished as if she feared he would change his mind.

His phone started to ring a second time. This time, he answered it. 'Hello, sir. Sorry, I was in the shower.'

'Those details you gave us about the journalist... We just hacked into his email account. He is on his way to Bangkok, touching down at two this afternoon. I will message the name of the hotel he's booked himself into. Stay away from him, okay?' The phone line was disconnected.

'What the fuck?' Jamie cursed loudly. How on earth could that asshole have known he was in Bangkok? He banged his fist on the table, which vibrated like it had caught a cold. Jamie regretted not killing Vicks in the airport manager's office. He'd refrained because his boss didn't like all these killings, but whenever he followed his boss's instructions, he ended up screwing up like this.

But as he thought more about it, he started to relax. Perhaps this twist wasn't bad news after all. What could a journalist do to him? He was sure Vicks had no weapons and no control whatsoever over the police in Thailand. And Jamie had done nothing wrong here.

The text from his boss arrived just then, and he read the name of the small hotel. He had no idea where it was, but he would find out. In the end, he decided to wait a couple of days, let Vicks keep searching for him. There was nothing that would lead to him, and he could relax. It felt nice to be ahead in this game of hide and seek.

CHAPTER 42

AFTER TWO THAIJITOS, Vicks paid up. He used cash to pay, not credit card, as he didn't want to leave a trail. By that time, he had learned a great deal about the bartender, Boon-Mee. He left him a five hundred Baht tip too. That was a lot for Vicks, but anything less might have looked inappropriate, given the usual clientele of The Peninsula.

Before getting up, he signaled for Boon-Mee to come over and pointed at the printout of Jamie's picture, which he'd placed on the table. 'Have you seen my friend? This is his picture. He said he would meet me here, but I haven't seen him.'

Thankfully, Boon-Mee played along. He looked at the A4-size sheet closely and said, 'No.' Then he added, 'But sir, if I see him, I can call you. Please give me your number.'

Vicks got to his feet and said, 'No, I will check back later. It is not that important. He has my number, and I'm sure he will call me.'

Boon-Mee nodded and escorted him out of the bar, and Vicks thanked him before moving on. A waste of money and time, he thought, as he walked out of The Peninsula hotel. Outside, he hopped into a waiting tuk-tuk and headed for the Mandarin Oriental, wondering as he went if there was a better way.

CHAPTER 43

SEATED FIVE TABLES away, Ariel had observed Vicks' every move. He had been careful to keep Vicks from being able to get a good look at him and had, therefore, taken a table with an obstructed view. Whenever he wanted, he could twist his neck to check on Vicks, but when he was upright, if Vicks had turned, all he would have seen was a thicket of bamboo shrubs.

Ariel followed Vicks out of The Peninsula hotel. He was a concerned man at the moment. If he stayed too close to Vicks, Vicks would eventually realize that he was being followed. On the other hand, if he increased the distance, there was every chance of losing sight of Vicks altogether.

CHAPTER 44

VICKS WALKED INTO the Mandarin Oriental. He had looked back a few times and was aware of seeing the same face several times. But he was not one hundred percent sure if the man was indeed following him. It was a face he had never seen before. Could be a coincidence, he thought, as he wandered through the opulent lobby and headed towards the bar.

The bamboo bar was straight out of an African safari. Decorated with big leopard prints, it spread around him like an amoeba under a bright golden-yellow ceiling.

By that point, Vicks was hungry, so he ordered a plate of chicken satay, calling the bartender by his name and accepting his offer to try the house specialty, an Oriental Mai Tai, which he explained contained Thai rum in place of the Cuban brown rum in the standard mai tai.

He sipped the drink and looked around. It was time to again chat up the bartender. But he wondered how long could he go on like this. By the time he visited the third bar, he would be tipsy enough that he'd have to head back to the hotel and crash. The night would bring better opportunities, he thought. He had planned to hit the red light district and the sleazy bars adjoining it. Talk to the cab drivers, the waitresses, even the pimps; he hoped someone would recall Jamie.

But this adventure could put him in a tight spot. Vicks didn't mind tight spots, but only when there was no threat to his life. He knew that visiting the areas frequented by the scum of society with the picture of a murderer in his hand wasn't a sane thing to do. He thought about Tonya and once again considered giving up the job of an investigative reporter.

But that would be proving his father right. That would also be tarnishing the memory of his mother and the promise he had made that day, staring into the funeral pyre, that he would do things right, that he would be brave. Never a sissy.

Vicks felt the futility of what he was doing and thought how rudderless his boat was at the moment. The tide under his boat was taking him in an unknown direction.

The food soothed some of his nerves. He felt saner once he'd eaten and bathed in the luxury around him, a bit spoilt.

In his peripheral vision, he saw a man walk towards him and stop near his table. Before Vicks could look up, the man slid into the chair opposite.

'Hello, Mr. Vicks.'

The voice was familiar, and it took Vicks a second to recognise him. Seated in front of him was the man he had come to Bangkok for. Jamie was totally at ease, wearing a fashionable suit and a confident, know-it-all smile.

CHAPTER 45

JAMIE HAD SEEN Vicks walk into the Bamboo bar, where he was sitting in the corner nursing a drink, just killing time. He had called Suzy, but an appointment with the lap dancer couldn't be arranged for before ten that night. It was just as well, as he was still spent from the surprise gift he had found in his bed early that morning. She had been an exceptional lay, and he was wondering exactly when he went down to pick her up last night.

When Vicks walked in, Jamie blinked again and again, not believing his eyes. Still not sure, he bit his finger to convince himself that he wasn't dreaming. The goat had walked in front of the tiger of its own free will. This was as good as anybody's luck could get. Or as bad, if he thought about it from Vicks' perspective. When Vicks turned to look around, Jamie ducked out of sight.

As Vicks got busy ordering his drink, Jamie decided to use the element of surprise, just like last time. But unlike in Udaipur, he would not be able to attack Vicks after the surprise. There were people around, and (he checked discreetly) at least one camera covered the area where Vicks sat. Jamie thought about it for a while, and a plan began to take shape in his mind.

He went up to his room and returned five minutes later with a powerful sedative that he kept in reserve for emergencies like this. It was a tasteless and colourless fast-dissolving tablet. Now all he had to do was wait, his eyes on the bar. Luckily for him, Vicks was seated on a sofa chair about twenty feet from the bar.

As soon as the waiter left his tray on the counter top and rounded the entire length of the bar to come pick it up, Jamie walked across to where the tray was sitting. He placed his hands on the shiny surface, ensured that his back blocked the camera, and dropped the pill into the high ball glass containing Vicks' cocktail. Then he moved quickly away before Vicks spotted him.

When the bartender returned after serving the drink to Vicks, Jamie asked for his scotch to be refilled. He smiled at his reflection in the mirror to his left and sipped his scotch. He needed to wait for about ten minutes for the drug to start working. When he thought it was time, Jamie got up and parked himself across from Vicks, a smile on his face.

The journalist was shocked. He had been looking for Jamie, had come this close to finding him, but his luck had run out.

'Welcome to Bangkok, my dear friend.'

Jamie waited for a reply, watching Vicks struggle to speak. For a moment, he was not sure if it was shock that was keeping him wordless or the pill that had turned his voice box to jelly. When more than ten seconds elapsed and Vicks kept staring at him, his eyes a shade droopy, Jamie knew his prey had turned into a vegetable.

He called the bartender over. 'My friend here is not feeling well. He needs rest. Can you help me get him up?'

'Sure.' The bartender helped Jamie, and they were able to get Vicks to his feet.

'I need to take him to his room.'

'Wait, I will call for first aid. We have a doctor too. He will be here in less than ten minutes.'

Jamie smiled and tried his best to play it cool. 'There is no problem. He's just tired. Once he's had some rest, he'll be fine. I just need a wheelchair.'

The bartender was back in a minute from a room close by. Large hotels always kept wheelchairs handy near reception desks and bars for emergencies exactly like this. Jamie lowered Vicks into the chair, thanked the bartender, and pushed Vicks away.

In less than three minutes, they were in Jamie's room. He spun the chair and smiled as the wheelchair turned around and brought Vicks face to face with him. Jamie closed the door, pulled a chair over, and sat down across him.

'First, why are you following me?' he asked, a serious expression on his face, the lid on his anger about to blow off. But Vicks didn't reply. The drug had crippled him. 'Okay, we will wait. The effect will begin to wear off in four hours.'

CHAPTER 46

ARIEL WAS FLUMMOXED by developments. From a distance, he'd seen an immobile Vicks being wheeled out of the bar and taken towards the lifts. Instead of following them, he chose to talk to the bartender first. He was sure the man pushing the wheelchair was Jamie, but he was also sure that Jamie would not be foolish enough to kill a journalist like Vicks in a five-star hotel. That would be signing his own death warrant. Perhaps he wanted to find out how much Vicks knew about him and throw a scare into Vicks so he'd let Jamie alone in the future.

Jamie had killed Sherry Bing. In cold blood. There seemed to be no motive except the fact that she was waiting for Ariel. By that point, Ariel also knew that Jamie had been in love with Sherry. He felt a rare wave of anger surge in his veins.

When he came face to face with the barman, Ariel brought his emotions under control and smiled. 'I am concerned about the man who has just been taken by that gentleman to his room.'

'I am not surprised, sir. I'm used to seeing all sorts of weird things happen to tourists in Bangkok. They drink like fish and take drugs to enhance their libidos for their orgies and what not. We just put up with

them. Our job is to watch, not react.' The bartender
seemed worked up.

'Do you think those two are friends?'

'Yes, because the man who helped him said so. If
they weren't friends, why would he help him?'

'Right, I am a doctor and have some time. Do you
think I should go check on him?'

'Sure, sir.'

'Which room was he taken to?'

The bartender showed him the slip that Jamie had
signed. Ariel was surprised by the name. According to
the slip, the name was Daniel Alphonso. Room 1402.

Ariel made a mental note of the name and headed
for the reception desk. After looking around, he called
his boss in Tel Aviv. This was a curious development,
and he needed access to the Thai intelligence service.
His boss assured him of help on top priority. Ariel sat
down to wait, allowing the secret services of the two
nations to cooperate with each other. It could take an
hour, and if he was unlucky, maybe even four. In the
meantime, Vicks' life was in danger.

More questions began to pop into his mind. How
on earth did Vicks guess that Jamie was to be found in
the Mandarin Oriental? Or was this a planned meeting?
Were the two of them on the same side? Ariel knew he
needed to be patient for a while longer.

CHAPTER 47

ACROSS THE ROAD in a café sat ACP Rao. He had arrived in Bangkok a few hours before and was keeping track of Vicks via his Delhi office. As soon as Vicks called Tonya, the Delhi police had started to monitor his number. The ACP was getting constant updates and knew Vicks' position in real time, with an accuracy of around twenty-five meters. But the trouble came in tall buildings, like the one Vicks was in at that moment. The tracking system could not detect the height. As long as a person was in the same geographical position and his latitude and longitude didn't change, his position would appear to remain the same, whether he was on the ground floor or the fortieth. So ACP Rao had seen that Vicks' position had changed once since he arrived but was now steady in a new position.

ACP Rao emailed the latitude and longitude to Delhi to find out where Vicks was at the moment. He got a reply in a few moments. The position corresponded to the hotel's underground parking garage. What was Vicks doing in the parking garage? He had remained in the same position for the past half hour. Was he waiting for someone? Was he in trouble?

ACP Rao paid for his coffee, which he hadn't even touched, and approached the hotel cautiously. He reached the underground parking garage and advanced to Vicks' position, pausing behind each pillar to make sure he was not seen. But when he finally reached the place Vicks was supposed to be, he didn't see any sign of him. ACP Rao's first thought was that Vicks had learned he was being followed and abandoned his phone. But when he searched everywhere and didn't find the phone, he became worried. He looked up. Vicks could be in the same position on any of the fifty-odd floors above his head. ACP Rao kicked a crushed cola can that was lying nearby.

He thought about the Israeli agent who had come to meet the Police Commissioner in Delhi. The ACP had hatched the idea of letting the Israelis into the fray, as the more eyes looking for the enemy the better. ACP Rao took Ariel's photograph out of his pocket and wondered where he was. Was he also in Bangkok?

After briefly going over the options available to him, the ACP left the parking area and entered the lobby of the Mandarin Oriental. He spotted Ariel lounging near the reception desk. ACP Rao had nothing to worry about, as they had never met, so being recognized wasn't a possibility.

Ariel glanced at him as ACP Rao walked in and sat in a chair about four feet from him.

What was he doing here, ACP Rao thought, seemingly so much at ease?

After half an hour, he saw a man from the reception desk approach Ariel and whisper something. The man's mannerisms gave his intentions away—he was passing some confidential information. Ariel nodded and was escorted by the man to a room right behind the reception desk. ACP Rao waited. Something was brewing.

CHAPTER **48**

'YOU FOOL, THE Israelis already *have* the information we expected *you* to intercept after Sherry Bing received it.'

Never before, even when angry, had Jamie's boss had such a chilling effect on him. He held the phone tightly against his ear, unable to defend himself. All the money spent by his boss and the time and resources expended by Jamie in wooing Sherry had been a waste. Because when the time came, Jamie had failed to recover the message she had traveled from Udaipur to Delhi for.

'But boss, I swear she had nothing on her,' Jamie meekly offered.

There was silence on the other end of the line, and then his boss started to laugh. Jamie was surprised. 'Jamie, I must tell you that you are doing a good job. The information she was waiting to receive was planted by our operatives. It was we who sent the message to her.'

'What? What was my role, then?'

'You were meant to make things difficult for her, so that when she did pass the information to her country, her struggle to fight you would add to the information's appearance of being genuine.'

'So I was just space filler.'

'No, I wouldn't put it that way. You were on an official assignment.'

Taking advantage of the pause, Jamie decided to change the subject. He would mull over the details his boss had provided later. 'Boss, I have Vicks in my room. I have immobilized him. What do I do with him?'

He heard his boss take a long breath. 'Have a conversation with him, tell him clearly that you will kill him, and then let him overpower you and escape. In your conversation, tell him that Iran has chemical weapons stored and ready to use at a secret location and plans to fire missiles at Tel Aviv from the sea in a few days.'

'Yes, boss, but what will we gain by it?'

But his boss had disconnected.

Jamie looked at Vicks and smiled. It would be another hour before he woke. Jamie got up and tied Vicks' hands behind the chair, leaving the knot a little loose so that, with some struggle, it could come off. Then he placed his pistol on the table close to Vicks, setting it down as far from himself as he could. Satisfied with the arrangement, he sat down to wait.

He began to think about what his boss had said. From what he understood, Iran had wanted to pass some information to Israel in such a manner that they would believe it beyond any doubt. And to add to this believe quotient, they had used Jamie. He remembered that his boss had gotten annoyed when he killed Sherry Bing. But how could he have known what the real game was?

As he thought more about it, the new development began to gnaw at him, causing irritation and increasing his temper. Because of the Iranian intelligence agency's little game, he had killed someone he had begun to love. His own agency had used him.

Jamie felt a tightening in his chest. He opened a miniature scotch bottle from the mini bar and drank it in one gulp. The alcohol swam inside his body in its enthusiasm to mingle with his blood. Within a few minutes, he felt the kick. But the effect was far from soothing.

Sherry was not a Muslim, but that didn't condemn her to an early death. She was at the hotel that morning not because she wanted to be, but because she was fooled into believing something by Jamie's boss.

He downed another miniature scotch. She'd been in love with him. He'd loved her too. Perhaps he could have persuaded her to change her religion. He had never seen her pray, so it could have been possible. There were millions of people in the world who prioritized love over religion. But the poor thing was history now. Jamie threw the empty miniature bottle against the wall and opened another one. Then he abused his boss at the top of his voice. For the first time, Jamie began to doubt whether the biggest decision of his life—the one to serve Islam—had been the right one. He had simply become a puppet in the hands of some really nasty people.

There was a knock. Jamie peeped through the keyhole and, on not seeing anyone, asked, 'What do you want?'

'Room service.'

'Fuck you. Can't you see the *Do Not Disturb* sign hanging outside?'

'Sir, we need to check your bathroom. There is a serious leak in the room directly below yours. We sincerely apologize for the inconvenience.'

'Fuck off. I won't open.'

Jamie returned to his chair. The person outside was definitely not hotel staff. Jamie had been to Thailand enough times to spot a genuine Thai twang when a local spoke English. Who was outside?

At that moment, Vicks stirred in his chair. He was about to regain consciousness.

Jamie decided to toe the line set by his boss for the time being. Backing out had serious consequences, and he wasn't prepared to take such a risk. He would have his revenge on his boss for keeping him in the dark later. If the details about the chemical weapons could be shared by his boss now, they could have been shared earlier.

'You?' Vicks slurred through the question, his expression showing fear.

'Take it easy, Mr. Journalist. How are you feeling? I had to engage in this little circus because you wouldn't have come with me on your own.'

'What do you want?'

'Well, I think that's my question.'

'You are a criminal; you murdered an innocent woman in Delhi.'

'And now I'm going to murder you. But before you die, I want you to know that Iran has enough chemical weapons to attack Israel, India's nasty little friend, and we will do it very soon. That woman learned our little secret and had to die. Just as you know it now, and therefore, I have no choice but to kill you.'

Jamie was impressed by this journalist, who had the guts to speak like that when he was totally restrained and about to die. But he had no appetite for killing him. And disposing off his body in a secure luxury hotel would be a real issue. The boss had also asked him not to.

Jamie wondered how much longer it would take for the man before him to free himself and dash for the door. When that happened, he would jump after him and deliberately miss the escaping man.

And minutes later, he would check out and once again be an anonymous man on the roads of Bangkok.

He thought of the woman who gave him a lap dance last night, and his stress eased.

CHAPTER 49

AS VICKS LISTENED to Jamie, fear gripped him. This man was talking about killing thousands of innocent people using weapons of mass destruction. Though he knew Iran had been trying to build nuclear weapons, that they were also making chemical warheads was news to him.

As a well-informed journalist who had taken his history lessons at journalism school seriously, he knew that during the Iran-Iraq war of the eighties, Iraq had used mustard, nerve, and sarin gases against Iran. These attacks had annihilated over a hundred thousand Iranian soldiers and civilians and proved to be the turning point in the war. At that time, Iran didn't possess any chemical weapons, and therefore, it couldn't retaliate.

If Iran had developed chemical weapons now, it was only a logical progression of the unfinished business in the region. It was also common knowledge that America had helped Iraq to develop the chemical artillery that was used against Iran and that the scientists backing the project had been mostly Jewish.

As a journalist, this was a dream scoop for Vicks. He would bring in the historical perspective and the story would make headlines all over the world after *India Now* published it. But he also knew that this secret information had been fed to him because he was about to be killed. The thought deflated his excitement, and the nearness of certain death pressed the panic button inside him.

He could hear someone in the corridor outside. Vicks wanted to shout for help, but that would only ensure that the enemy lost his cool and killed him instantly. Maybe Vicks could reason with the killer. But what could he say? As he was mulling over his options, he realized that he was able to move his wrists, which were tied behind him, a little. Jamie had gone into the bathroom, and Vicks tried harder to move his hands. Within a few minutes, the knot was undone. Vicks' hands were free now, but he held onto the rope. If it fell to the carpet, Jamie would notice it and block his way to the door. Jamie was better built, and even with free hands, there was little chance that Vicks could knock him over and make it out the door.

It was at that moment that he noticed the pistol. From this angle, he could also see that the magazine was inserted. The weapon seemed to be ready. All he had to do was grab the gun, cock it, and point it at the bathroom door. He heard the sound of running water stop.

The decision had to be made without delay. Vicks dropped the rope, jumped towards the pistol, and stood up after cocking the gun, all in under two seconds. Just at that moment, Jamie emerged from the bathroom. His eyes widened.

'Whoa, whoa... Careful with that.'

'Get out of my way.'

Jamie stepped to one side, and Vicks dashed for the door. In his peripheral vision, he saw Jamie lunge at him desperately. His left hand hit Vicks' thigh, but before he could recover, Vicks was out of the room. As he ran, the pistol fell from his hand. But there was no turning back now.

He ran into another man in the corridor, shoving him into the wall. Before the ice in his veins could thaw, Vicks sped away, taking the stairs. He jumped down three at a time, and when he had descended about five floors, he finally slowed, trying to listen to the sound of his heartbeats.

He heard feet rushing downstairs, maybe about two floors up. Vicks opened a door and entered a corridor, wondering where to go next. Since he didn't have a room key, he knew he couldn't access the lift. But right at that moment, he saw the doors of the lift open and an old woman enter it. Vicks ducked in after her. There was no one else in the lift.

'Are you all right?' The old woman was squinting at him, adjusting her spectacles to observe him better.

'Yes... I was working out in the gymnasium,' Vicks explained.

The old woman nodded, but she didn't seem to be entirely convinced. After placing her room key next to the sensor, she pressed the button marked *Lobby*.

As the doors began to close, Vicks heard someone dashing for the lift. A man's face came into view, but by then the doors had almost closed. Vicks got a good look at the man's face and saw that it was the same man who had followed him to both the hotels in which he'd searched for Jamie.

When the doors opened in the lobby, Vicks stepped out. He hurried across to the front door but didn't run. He couldn't risk being stopped and investigated. There were people everywhere, and soft music was playing. In seconds, he was out of the hotel and on the sidewalk, his swift feet taking him away from the place where he was almost killed. He was lucky to escape by the skin of his teeth.

Vicks walked about a hundred meters before he hopped inside a tuk-tuk that slowed near him.

'Hello, Vicks Menon,' said the man already seated inside as the tuk-tuk began to gain speed.

Vicks had heard this voice before, and his heartbeat stopped. It belonged to the killer. He had not been able to outrun him. He had failed yet again.

CHAPTER 50

VICKS TURNED TO face the voice. The man seated next to him was smiling. It wasn't the killer, Jamie. It was ACP Rao. Vicks took a few moments to calm down the whirling in his head.

The recognition brought relief. Here was someone at last, in a foreign land, that he could trust.

'Hi, ACP Rao. You indeed are the real police, always at work after everything is over.'

'But this is not a movie, Vicks. This is real. Where were you in the hotel?'

By now, the shock had subsided and Vicks' ability to reason was restored. ACP Rao, though a good police officer, couldn't be trusted with all the information. Yes, his men had freed Vicks from that lousy toilet in the airport manager's office in Udaipur, but this time, Vicks had made his escape all by himself. He now had a scoop of a story, and it was difficult for him to keep that from showing.

But before he could decide how much to tell ACP Rao, he wanted to know what the policeman was doing in Bangkok. How did he learn that Vicks was at the hotel? This could not be a coincidence. 'First, ACP Rao, I want to know what you're doing here.'

'You told me that. Remember?' He paused, and after Vicks nodded, continued, 'Look, I was just tailing you for your own safety.'

'But you didn't save me when I needed you the most. That bastard was about to kill me in that room.'

For a moment, the ACP looked shocked. The expression vanished quickly and he said, 'Well, I was keeping a safe distance. I didn't want to scare you off. And besides, there was someone else on your tail.'

Vicks nodded. 'I spotted that man too. In fact, when I escaped, he was right outside the room I was being held in. I heard his voice, and I also ran into him. Who the hell is he?'

The tuk-tuk stopped.

ACP Rao gestured for Vicks to get out. They headed down the sidewalk, which was dotted with shops. A group of Japanese tourists clutching tour books and listening intently to a tour guide, who held up a small pole with a pennant on it, passed them. They let them pass and resumed walking after a minute.

'The man in the hotel is an Israeli intelligence operative.'

Vicks thought about the information he had obtained about Iran's plan to attack Israel using chemical weapons. 'Israeli?'

'I don't know. We know that Sherry Bing was an Israeli citizen. But why is their intelligence service tailing you? To the best of my understanding, they think you will lead them to the killer of Sherry Bing.'

They ducked into a Thai restaurant. It was a regular, cheap joint, with numerous people eating and gossiping and a lot of steam escaping through the open kitchen. When Vicks refused any food, ACP Rao ordered Thai green curry with Jasmine rice.

ACP Rao stared into Vicks' eyes and said, 'Tell me everything that has happened. I am not a policeman here, Vicks; I am a man just like you, with no immunity and in equal danger. I don't even have a weapon.'

'But you could call the Thai police, and you have your ID to prove who you are. So you are different.'

'Okay, but at the moment, I am like you. If you share everything with me, I will be in a better position to help you. Tell me who you were running away from. What happened in the hotel?'

Vicks took a deep breath and started to speak slowly, his brain eliminating what was not necessary.

'Jamie drugged me and took me to his room. He was about to kill me, but I was lucky and escaped.'

The food arrived, and the smell made Vicks hungry too. But he asked for a coffee instead. ACP Rao didn't even look at his food. He spoke through the steam that rose between the two of them: 'Thank God you escaped. What else do you know about this Jamie guy, and why did he kill that poor woman in Delhi? Did he say anything to you?'

'He is an Iranian intelligence agent, and he killed her because he suspected her of hiding something in that hotel. It was the same man who knocked me out cold in Udaipur.'

Vicks decided to tell him no more. That was enough to repay whatever ACP Rao had done for him. The policeman seemed satisfied with the information and began to eat. Vicks picked up his cup of coffee.

Chapter 51

JAMIE WAS SMILING like a kid on Eid as he closed the door of his room. Placing the pistol near Vicks had been a big risk. What if the guy panicked and fired? He'd known it was possible and that the risk he was taking was greater than the reward. But sometimes, if one played along with one's instincts, he mused, things worked out fine. Like now.

He packed quickly. His best guess was that, even if Vicks got his wits together, it would be at least two hours before anyone came knocking at his door. Well before that time, maybe in less than half an hour, he would be out of danger. His plan was simple—to get as far from the Mandarin Oriental as possible. Bangkok was a crazy city, always hungry to absorb those who needed hiding. It was a playground for thousands of wanted criminals from all over the world.

Jamie opened his door and peeped outside. The corridor was empty. He had been worried about the man Vicks had run into while fleeing his room. Jamie had seen the man's face only briefly before he turned and ran after Vicks. Who was he and why had he gone after Vicks? One thing was amply clear, however. The man's target was Vicks, not Jamie, and therefore, he had nothing to worry about at the moment.

A quick-descending lift brought him to the lobby, and he walked through perfumed air and music to the reception desk. Five minutes later, he was in the backseat of a cab moving through the slow traffic of Bangkok. He had followed his boss's instructions to the letter, and now it was time to do some serious thinking. Jamie was no longer smiling, as he'd experienced a tectonic shift in his conscience. It was clear to him that his own agency had used him. He recalled the phone conversation with his boss an hour ago and felt even guiltier for murdering Sherry Bing.

If he chose to quit, could he, at thirty, get a job? A job would not be difficult to find, but would it come with a flexible schedule, boundless fun, and unlimited access to pleasure? He knew that the answer was *no*. Regular employment wouldn't be exciting at all, for several reasons. One, Jamie would have to assume his real identity of Jalaluddin. Two, work his ass off in London, take the tube to work every day, and survive a boss who would be breathing down his neck to achieve impossible sales targets. Three, go to mosque every Friday. Four, stay away from alcohol and women. And five, eat only halal meat. Even the thought of leading such a life was nauseating. He was used to living the life of a Christian, and the identity of Jamie was no longer alien to him.

A regular job would be a disaster. He had dived too deep into this shit, chasing his Muslim duty, and there was no chance of turning back now. He stared blankly out the window and waited for the taxi to reach Khaosan Road, the backpacker's ghetto, where hotel owners were discreet and escape was blink-of-an-eye quick when required.

***

A car followed Jamie's, a lone passenger in the backseat reading a newspaper. The man patted the driver's shoulder when the car ahead came to a stop. After he had seen his target enter a small hotel, the man got out. He read the faded name board: Angong Guesthouse. He looked up at the three-story building, keeping behind a tree that marked one of its corners. It seemed perfect for people looking to fade away from attention.

The man got himself a hat and extra-large sunglasses from a shop close by and decided to wait at a tea shop across the road.

CHAPTER 52

ALPHA PUT THE phone down and smiled. There was every reason for him to be at ease. Jamie, his errant pupil, had delivered at last. The journalist had been fed the right information.

Alpha had been given his name in school. He was a good student of physics and mathematics, and his jealous friends had named him Alpha. The name stuck with him. He liked the sound of it, and also the fact that it meant number one.

Alpha looked out the window. Dawn was just breaking in Tehran, and Milad tower was seemingly eager to puncture the sky to the north, its stick-with-a-bulb-on-top structure becoming more visible through the dark with every passing second.

Killing that woman in Delhi had been a mistake. He had never ordered Jamie to kill her; he had only been required to take the letter after she received it. Not because Alpha needed the letter, but because he wanted her to be convinced that the information in it was important. He wanted to make sure she took the information to the enemy. To the Israelis. He lost his composure all of a sudden and banged his fist on the table. Just the thought of the Israelis made his blood boil.

Sherry Bing had been the bait.

Alpha had trusted Sherry Bing to be intelligent, like her father. He had expected her to make a copy when she received the message. Before Jamie came to grab it from her. But something had gone wrong. The man with the letter didn't reach her in time, and an overzealous pupil had killed her. He felt the anger but didn't hit the table this time. Jamie was young, and the young sometimes committed mistakes without intending them.

Sherry's father was still in Alpha's custody, right there in Tehran. They had tortured him, but the old man hadn't cracked. Finally, drugs mixed with his food did the trick. The drugs played with his head, and within days, he'd revealed an address and a password. Using the drugs was dangerous, as there was a risk of the old man dying of an overdose. But when nothing else worked on the stubborn Israeli, Alpha had turned to drugs with a prayer in his heart. God had heard him.

After that, the operation went smoothly. Early one morning, Alpha sent one of his men to the other Israeli spy disguised as Sherry's father. The password confirmed his identity, and the other man agreed to become a messenger.

Alpha had killed two birds with one stone. One, he'd showed the door to an Israeli spy, who left Tehran fearing for his life. And two, the man had set off to do an errand for the Iranians without his knowledge, delivering a misleading message.

But Sherry's murder changed everything. And the message had never reached her. Which meant the enemy didn't have the information that they should have had. That also meant Iran didn't have the leverage.

But now, that mistake had been undone. The journalist was pregnant with the information, and once he gave it to the Indians, the Israelis would have it in no time. He knew that India and Israel were close allies. But still, one part of the puzzle was missing. Where was the man who was sent with the message? Alpha's best guess was that he must have been killed while traveling through the lawless parts of Pakistan. But assumptions had no place in his line of work. He would have to find out more.

He picked up the phone that sat before him on the well-polished teakwood table. It was a direct hotline. 'The bird's taken the bait. But the messenger still remains elusive.'

There was no sound, except breathing, to show someone was there.

Then the call was disconnected. Alpha had been working for the Iranian intelligence service, or VAJA as everyone knew it, for over thirty-five years now. He was one of the first foot soldiers, who got the job soon after the Islamic revolution of 1978. He had hated the Shah who brought the country down.

He was one of those in the crowd of millions who cheered the return of Ayatollah Khomeini after living in exile for nineteen years. And finally, when he said in the form that he filled out after college that he wanted to work to keep Iran's enemies at bay, they gave him this job. They would have put him in the military, but he had by then lost one of his legs after a street fight against the Shah's supporters. The knife wound never healed, and when his father finally had enough money to take him to the doctor, the leg had to be cut off.

In the last thirty-five years, Alpha had done much to be proud of. And this was his last mission before he retired and walked away to the Alborz Mountains north of Tehran to live a quiet life in his tiny village, eating Chelow kabab, the favorite dish of most Iranians.

CHAPTER 53

VICKS DECIDED TO return home, as there was nothing left for him to do in Bangkok. He felt a rare satisfaction, as this assignment had turned out to be his most successful investigative work so far. Now he not only knew the motive of the killer but also had information that could easily become the scoop of the decade.

But the trouble was how to handle the information about the chemical weapons. As he thought more about it, he realized that his instincts and the call of duty were at loggerheads. By publishing information about the chemical weapons, as was his journalistic duty, he would be sticking his neck too far out. Taking the lid off such matters could sometimes lead to a chain reaction, even a world war. It was frightening. Vicks thought about whistleblowers. Not just their nerves but their brains must be made of steel. He was not sure, though, if he possessed the will to spill the beans about Iran's plan to attack Israel with chemical weapons. It needed deeper thought and analysis.

His instinct urged him to turn to Tonya. He could always count on her to brighten his day. But speaking over the phone would increase his risk. He would have to play it safe for the moment. ACP Rao had told him that they were tracking Tonya's phone. The police would know anything he told her instantly.

The Vortex, he had thought until now, was caused by the police looking for a scapegoat. Someone unlucky enough to be caught in the crossfire, simply at the wrong place at the wrong time. The police chased such people like hounds on performance-enhancing drugs. But what he was experiencing at the moment was new. Vicks had been sucked into *The Vortex*, but it wasn't due to the police. It was his free will, his desire to chase a good story. His conscience had become *The Vortex*. He had trapped himself.

ACP Rao had bid him farewell after their meeting in the restaurant, asking him to return to India. He said he would share some details with the Thai police, visit the Mandarin Oriental, take some fingerprints, and collect strands of hair for a DNA profile to compare with international records. Basically, routine police business. Vicks had nodded and said he would return to the hotel to pick up his stuff, then go to the airport.

After reaching his B&B in Bangkok, Vicks unlocked his room and went in, where he sat with his face resting in his cupped palms. He was looking out the small window without seeing anything in particular. His thoughts were on the story. How to filter the information and give out something substantial, yet limited enough to avoid being sucked deeper into *The Vortex*.

He opened his laptop after ten minutes and began to type.

The killer is on the loose in Bangkok, which he reached from Udaipur by a route not known. He checked in at the Oriental Mandarin, a luxury hotel, under the name of Daniel Alphonso. The hotel's staff says the man seems to have a drinking problem. Before Delhi police could capture him, he fled from the hotel, and his whereabouts are unknown. It is understood that the Delhi police are seeking the Thai police's cooperation and are close on his heels.

An investigation carried out by India Now has revealed that the killer murdered Sherry Bing in Paharganj. In India, he was living under the assumed identity of 'Jamie'. As reported earlier, the victim was in love with him. According to one source, the victim had learned a very damaging secret about the killer.

While the victim was a Jew, it is unknown if Jamie was as well. Jamie's real name remains unknown. The question is, did he kill his lover because she was a Jew? What had she learned about him?

Vicks continued to wonder if he should add the dangerous part: that Iran was about to attack Israel with chemical warheads. That little piece would catapult *India Now* to the top. But it would also increase the pressure on his boss to reveal the source of this information. His boss, he knew, would point the finger at Vicks in no time. Yet he thought it was his duty to share this news with the people and government officials, so that pressure could be placed on Iran. If he added this explosive scoop, his own life could be in grave danger. And if he didn't, the lives of many more would be in danger. It was his life versus the lives of thousands of other innocents.

Vicks pressed his palms tightly against his temples. The pressure eased some of the sudden pain that had shot through his head, but it could do nothing to change the reality surrounding him.

CHAPTER 54

WEARING A HAT and extra-large sunglasses, Ariel had been watching the Angong guesthouse in the Khaosan area of Bangkok for over five hours now. There had been no sign of Jamie, which was odd. Was he resting?

He shared this with his boss over the phone and was given a name and phone number. Ariel called the number, and the man he spoke to arrived half an hour later. He was short and squat, like most Thais, and wore a flashy orange shirt and green cargo shorts, as if he was on holiday. He was smoking a cigarette and smiled at Ariel as he extended his hand.

On a police under cover job that required discretion, it was a bad choice of clothes. But thankfully, the man could speak mediocre English. Ariel knew that, in Thailand, mediocre was the best one could get.

After brief introductions, Ariel got down to business. 'Our target is in there... in Angong guesthouse. You know the target's name already, right?'

The man nodded. 'I have his picture too, Mister Man.' He removed the picture from one of the pockets of his cargo shorts and showed it to Ariel.

It was Ariel's turn to nod. The picture was of a younger Jamie. It appeared that the Thai police knew a lot more about Jamie than he did.

When the man spoke next, his hunch was confirmed. 'This man has been in our records for a few months now. But we have nothing concrete on him. He travels on fake British passports under a different name every time. Got it, Mister Man?'

'What's his business?'

'We suspect he is working for an intelligence service. But for which country... we don't know that yet.'

'He killed a woman in India last week. Why would he do that?'

'Too many questions, Mister Man.' He smiled and ran a relaxed hand over his bald head. Next, he stubbed the cigarette out with the determination of a firefighter and lit another one.

'Right.' That was the problem with policemen. Even while collaborating, they would treat each other with suspicion.

'Okay, Mister Man, I go in, you follow.'

'Sure, are you armed?'

'You think I am here on a holiday, Mister Man?'

Ariel failed to understand the man's confidence. Or was he trying to be humorous? In any case, Ariel reasoned, the man had volunteered to go in first. So he was protected.

They went into the hotel. In the ten by ten lobby, a young man with spiky hair chewed gum behind a small reception desk. A small TV hung on the wall to his right, and his eyes were glued to it. Until they came up and stopped in front of the small counter, the man with the spiky hair didn't take his eyes off it. Finally, he looked up, smiled, and spoke in Thai.

Ariel's Thai partner showed him the picture, and the man nodded enthusiastically. They had the room number in a minute, and after the Thai officer's police ID was shown, the young man handed over the master key as nervously as a tourist giving a valuable possession to an armed thief.

The room was on the second floor, and they took the wooden stairs. Ariel followed his partner, uncomfortable with the noise they were making. The wooden boards were old and creaked with each step. When they reached the second floor, the man took out a gun, and Ariel was relieved.

They slowed as they approached the room. The door was closed. The man placed his ear on the door panel and made a face in concentration. After a whole minute, he removed his head and smiled at Ariel.

'I can't hear a sound. The criminal is asleep. We will barge in now. I go in first and warn. Once I see his hands up, you come in and take his gun away. Okay?' he whispered.

So he was not such a fool after all, thought Ariel. He mouthed back soundlessly, 'Okay.'

Though the Thai policeman was clumsy in his approach, his clothes, and everything else, he finally got it right here. Silently, he turned the key and pushed open the door. Pistol first, he walked in, his knees slightly bent, his pupils dilated with the rush of adrenalin. Ariel watched him enter the room and pass out of sight. He stayed just outside the door, his ears focused on the room, thigh muscles flexing in anticipation.

And then he heard a cry of pain from inside. *Man down*, thought Ariel. He could do nothing at the moment, except run away if he wanted to save his life. His partner, who had the gun, had been overpowered. If he went inside to protect him, he would only make himself a sitting duck. This was no time for heroics.

The stairs were about twenty feet away, just six steps. He fled, no longer bothered by the amount of noise he was making, and jumped many stairs at a time to reach the lobby. Then he was out on the road.

But something made him stop.

'Hey, Mister Man,' called a familiar voice.

Vicks looked up and saw his partner on the balcony. He was smiling. The pistol wasn't visible anymore.

'Where are you running to, Mister Man?'

Ariel instantly understood the situation and returned to the hotel. When he entered the room, there was no sign of Jamie, and written across the wall were two words: *Fuck you*. It had been written by hand on an A4-size piece of paper and glued to the wall.

Ariel looked at his partner, who shrugged.

'Why did you cry out? I thought you were hurt,' Ariel asked.

'Silly, that is how we Thais yell when we are frustrated. Your man, our man... whatever... he is gone now, Mister Man.'

The man lit a cigarette and left the room abruptly, leaving Ariel in a small empty room on Khaosan Road.

CHAPTER 55

VICKS CHECKED OUT of the B&B and took the metro to the airport. He was thinking about saving some of the money his boss had paid out. He seemed to have reached a dead end, as far as this case was concerned. There would be no more money. He had a scoop, but he was not sure what to do with it.

He called up his boss briefly, using the last of his cash on a disposable SIM card, and shared what he had unearthed so far. The response from the other side was 'good' and nothing else. Which meant there was no assurance of getting his job back. Or any more money. He had saved about fifty thousand from the two lakh he had received from *India Now*, which could sustain him for a month if he lived frugally. By then, he hoped to figure something out.

Vicks emailed the story he had prepared earlier. The flight was still two hours away. He was seated close to a banner that read *Bar*. Vicks looked at the banner and bent his head to see what was behind it. The entrance was attractive, and he could see comfortable chairs and a well-stocked bar with bottles of all shapes and sizes. Vicks wanted to have a drink but decided against it.

His boss called him. 'Vicks, what you've sent to me is chicken feed. I don't understand. I thought you would get me more.'

'Boss, I—'

'I know, I know, you've spent all your time in Bangkok doing your favourite thing: drinking.'

Vicks hated the sarcasm and the accusatory tone but knew it was better to stay quiet.

'I want more.'

Vicks considered his money problems and said, 'Boss, I have more, but I can't give it to you... I mean we can't run it in our newspaper. It would spell disaster.'

'What are you saying? You have decided to withhold information from me, your boss, who gave you that job, paid you money?'

'Look, it's not what it sounds like... I mean, this information is really explosive. I wouldn't give it to anyone, not even Tonya.'

'Vicks, *India Now* needs big stories. We need sensation. We need something that can shake the whole fucking world.'

There was silence. Vicks saw a couple emerge from the bar, laughing and holding hands. They were in love and happy. And relaxed.

'Vicks, I always knew you had talent, but you are so conflicted in your head. Don't think about what is wrong and right, just give me the whole goddamn story. Now.'

'I will come straight there and meet you in your office. I'm at the Bangkok airport now.' Vicks hung up.

Someone had once said that pain produces maximum adrenalin. Perhaps they were wrong, as the conflict in Vicks' mind raised the adrenalin in his body like never before.

Without knowing what he was doing, Vicks got up, picked up his bag, and walked into the bar as if he was sleepwalking.

A Thai waitress came and stood next to him, her hip thrust to one side provocatively. She smiled and looked down at Vicks.

'Rum, please.'

'Thai rum?'

'Do you have Indian Rum?'

She nodded and brought him a glass. Vicks downed the first one straight and asked for a second.

He drank a total of five, but the whirling in his head didn't stabilize. It slowed, though. The danger surrounding the revelation now looked less severe and the world a lot safer.

Vicks barely made it to his flight in time. If there was one place he felt safest at the moment, it was thirty thousand feet above the ground, surrounded by passengers. No one could attack him here.

He hoped to have a solution to all his problems by the time the plane landed. He wanted a job. He wanted to handle the information about the chemical weapons properly. He wanted to stop drinking. And he wanted Tonya back in his life. Alcohol thrumming in his veins, he thought that all these wishes were achievable. Those were his last thoughts as the aircraft rose into the sky.

CHAPTER 56

ADMIRAL ARIK GOLAN, the Commander in Chief of the Israeli Navy, sat in his office and looked carefully at the piece of paper in his hands. He dropped it as if it could soil his fingers. Arik had suspected Iran of a wicked scheme for a long time but had secretly hoped that better sense would prevail. It was not to be.

Behind him, the Mediterranean Sea was aquamarine. The weather was jacket-cold, but in his room on the tenth floor of Israeli Naval headquarters, it was warm.

Israel had been on Iran's hitlist for a long time. They had targeted their players, their businesses, and their internal security. Attacking Israel with chemical weapons was the final straw to break the camel's back. But their intelligence service had been able to intercept and decipher the letter which gave them the exact location of the building outside Tehran where the chemical weapons were being manufactured.

His voice a deep rumble, Arik called his secretary and asked for an emergency meeting with his operational heads.

'Sir, at what time?'

'Now,' he barked, not believing his own rudeness. Something in his mind was fluttering like a leaf stuck on a window pane, desperate to fly away.

The plan was formed in an hour. Three of their missile boats would accompany the USS Ronald Reagan, a United States aircraft carrier. Their navigation and weapons readiness was reviewed. Sailing orders were signaled to the ships, with instructions to set sail from Eilat port on the Gulf of Aqaba in two hours. Once they were in position, he told them, fighter jets would be launched from the USS Ronald Reagan. The building in Iran containing the chemical weapons would be destroyed.

The PM's office had declared a state of emergency and the distribution of special suits had begun. Schools were shut down, markets closed, and people advised to stay indoors. The Israeli people had regularly practiced a heightened state of emergency, and therefore, the panic was insignificant.

Impending disaster taken care of, Arik Golan called for another meeting. This time of all his Chiefs of Staff.

'Sir, at what time?'

'Now,' he barked again, but this time without regret. He had a job to do, and how well he did that job would decide the fate of his nation and the next generation. The soldier in him came out, convincing him that pleasantries were no longer required. It was wartime. Fifteen minutes later, he marched on long legs to the conference room at the end of the corridor. Ten officers rose from their chairs and nodded to him. No one greeted him. This wasn't the time for pleasantries. They didn't have even a second to spare. The enemy's arsenal had to be destroyed on its own soil.

'We'll commence stage one as soon as this briefing is over. Everything is laid out in our strategic plans, and we've practiced it enough times. Let's do this.'

He got up and left, a scramble of feet behind him as his Chiefs of Staffs left the conference room in a hurry.

Back in his office, before he placed a call to the Defence Secretary to confirm that he had complied with all the orders that had been sent to him via special messenger, he paused to lift the picture of his family from his desk. A woman with deep-blue eyes and a girl and boy, both in their teens, smiled back at him.

He picked up the phone and, as soon as it was answered, said, 'Shalom, we are all set, sir.'

'Shalom. We shall win,' the Defence Secretary answered, his voice like sandpaper.

Admiral Arik hung up and walked across the room to look at himself in the mirror. The man facing him was dressed in a pristine white uniform with gold over the shoulders. He ran his fingers across the nameplate on the right side of his chest before pausing to adjust the wide spectrum of ribbons on the left.

He was confident of their plan. It was a surgical operation with a two-pronged strategy: one, to attack the factory manufacturing chemical weapons in Tehran, and two, attack the ships carrying the chemical weapons long before they could get into range to fire them into Israeli territory. He had confidence in the professionalism of his navy. Yet he knew he could not afford to underestimate the strength and guile of the enemy. He sat down in his chair again, his fingers absentmindedly drumming on the desk, deep in thought, his eyebrows pinched.

CHAPTER 57

BY THE TIME Vicks landed in Delhi, he had rediscovered his sobriety. Sometimes, the best course of action was to use logic and not think on behalf of others. He mulled this over and decided to pass the hazardous information on to his boss.

The decision about whether to publish it or not was his boss's problem. His boss was on the payroll of the newspaper, not Vicks, and his boss clearly knew what was in the best interests of the company. As far as Vicks was concerned, he had done the job for money; it was a freelance assignment, like a contract. He had done his bit, and what the contractor wished to do with the product now was entirely his decision.

He called Tonya from the airport. She was surprised, but after he answered her questions about his wellbeing, she sounded relaxed.

'I am on the way to your clinic.'

'No, I am home. Come straight here.'

Vicks was there in an hour. Her eyes welled up on seeing him, and he fought tears too. Finally, calm overtook them, and she began to prepare tea. He joined her in the small open kitchen to tell her about his trip.

'You think your kitchen might be bugged?'

She glanced over her shoulder and smiled. 'It might be. Please stay close, and let's play whisper- whisper.'

He wrapped his arms around her from behind and gently squeezed. He held her there, happy to be alive, lucky to be in love. When she began to resist his kissing her ear, Vicks said softly, 'You said whisper, didn't you?'

His breath on her neck and ear made her want him right there, in the kitchen. But she said, 'Whisper, not kissper.'

Vicks laughed at the silliness of it. After a few moments, he began to share all the details.

Initially, he thought he would leave out the part where he was captured by Jamie and incapacitated and how he'd escaped from the room, but in the end, he didn't. She was a psychologist, and he needed her help. He also told her about his boss and that he'd decided to tell him everything.

They carried their cups to the small dining table and sat down silently.

After five minutes, Tonya said, 'Your decision to share everything with the boss is okay, I think, and you should do it immediately. He is the one who has to decide what to do with it. Should things go wrong, you'll be in the clear. But about this killer... I'm thinking that something doesn't add up. A ruthless killer like him lets you get away?'

There was a pause as they looked at each other.

'Now that you mention it,' Vicks said, 'I think it's odd too. His pistol was close to me, and the rope was loose.'

'I need to think about this some more, compare my previous notes, etc. I think you should go to your boss and tell him everything.'

Half an hour later, Vicks was with his boss. As planned, he told him everything. Every single detail. And as he was speaking, he recorded the conversation on his cell phone secretly, just in case.

'Now, my balance of one lakh rupees.'

'Vicks, you have gone through a lot, I agree. And I promised, but I don't think this expense will be approved.'

Vicks got up to leave. The boss didn't stop him. At the door, Vicks turned and said, 'Please don't overuse the information. Overkill is bad journalism. But you already know that, don't you, sir?'

He left and closed the door.

CHAPTER 58

THE OLD MAN, Sherry Bing's father, escaped. He couldn't believe that what he had been planning for the past six months could be achieved so easily. But he did have inside help. Without it, he'd still be there. The prison was a living hell, and in thirty years, no one had ever escaped. He paused, his lank frame humped at the back, and turned to see the last moments of Milad tower that was visible against the darkening sky.

His inside helper had been generous. He had arranged to get the old man some money and a vehicle. The old man rushed to the arranged spot and found a van there, Red Cross painted on its side. He stepped inside, and the doors were closed. No one spoke to him. It wasn't necessary. A dull bulb burned inside, and there was a wash basin. He cleaned himself up as best as he could and put on new clothes and finally an apron.

After he had trimmed his beard, he found a thin face looking at him from the mirror. If it weren't for his eyes, he wouldn't have recognized himself. He had been so close to death that he had almost given up. And then God sent a messiah.

Now, finally, he was a free man, a man tasked with stopping a grave disaster. The old man had met his helper only twice, and not even once had that man showed him his face. He had just said, 'As your children in Israel need saving, our children in Iran need saving too. War never solves anything; it just sets the stage for the next war.' The words still echoed in his ears and warmed his heart. There were gods in the enemy ranks too.

The old man had nodded, and his escape plan had been explained to him in detail.

The vehicle was moving smoothly now. He had no idea where was he being taken. He just knew what he had to do. There was a small table on one side of the van with a container on it. He removed the lid and was enveloped by the aroma of spices and meat. The old man ate with boorish hunger.

He had been given the news of his daughter's murder a week ago. A newspaper clipping was pushed under the door, and a man read out the message from outside. The room was dark, and the old man had waited for daybreak when, every day, a beam of light one inch wide lit his small cell. He had clutched the paper and cried bitterly. His daughter, Sherry, the apple of his eye, was dead. He'd tried many times to convince himself that this news was false, only to break down even more. The old man's wife had died when Sherry was only five, and he had raised her on his own.

The van came to a stop. He was pulled out rather harshly, and his first thought was that it had all been a game, just a crazy Iranian general's idea to show him hope, feed him well, and then kill him. Some debased ritual of the enemy.

He looked up. There was another vehicle, this time a car. He was shown to the door, and he climbed in. Again, no one spoke to him. The car began to move. The old man turned his head to watch the van. It was speeding away from them, towards the city he had come from. So it might not really be a dream. The feeling of relief put him to sleep. His final thoughts were that his food had been poisoned and now they were taking him to be fed to wild animals. Another of those debased rituals.

Even in sleep, he was clutching the newspaper clipping. It was the only thing he'd brought with him from the jail while escaping.

CHAPTER 59

WHEN VICKS WOKE up, Tonya was not at his side. He had stayed at her flat for the night. He tiptoed to the living room and saw her sitting at the dining table, a laptop opened in front of her and a diary at hand. He watched her from the door to the bedroom. She looked lovely, serious in her dedication and concerned in her approach. He quietly walked past her and entered the kitchen. Now her back was towards him.

Would he be able to prepare tea for her without disturbing her? As soon as he lit the gas stove, Tonya turned and said, 'Good morning!'

'Oh, I didn't want to disturb you.'

Both were alarmed at the thud outside the door before Tonya relaxed and announced, 'Newspaper, *India Now*. The delivery man throws it up from below.'

'I'll get it.' He raced past her, and she settled back in her chair.

For Vicks, the front page news was a bolt from the blue. It read: *Iran about to attack Israel with chemical weapons.*

Vicks read quickly through the entire article. His boss had printed everything he'd said, word for word. He sat down heavily as Tonya took the newspaper from his hands and began to read.

She looked up after finishing. 'Vicks, he's mentioned your name too.'

'Bastard.'

There was the sound of a car stopping outside. Vicks got up and moved the curtain an inch to check. Two men in their forties climbed out of a black Ambassador and looked up at the building. One of them was consulting a paper slip in his hands. They were looking for an address. These men were looking for him. The paper in their hands, their cool demeanor, and their brisk strides as they neared the entrance of the building gave them away.

'It's the police, or the intelligence service, or some government guys... serious people.'

'But you have nothing to worry about. It was all done by your boss. Just tell them that.' She began to move towards the door.

Vicks stopped her. 'No, I will escape off the balcony. You tell them I was here during the night but left and won't return till evening.'

'Vicks, you can't be serious. You'll become a fugitive if you do that.'

'I've got to go. Do as I tell you. Please.'

Vicks moved to the balcony and looked down. The flat was on the second floor; he couldn't just jump off. There was a knock on the door. He climbed over the railing and grabbed the pipe next to it. After he managed to slither down half the height, he jumped. It was time to scoot, and he did just that.

Inside the house, Tonya opened the door and looked at the two men. 'Yes?'

'We are looking for Vicks Menon, reporter with *India Now*.'

'You missed him by about ten minutes.'

'Really? And when will he be back?'

'He said late evening. Is everything all right?'

'We want to search the house.'

'First I want to see the warrant.'

'Too many movies.' They walked past her, and Tonya raised her hands in surprise. She stayed where she was. The men were back in two minutes. 'Sorry to bother you.'

She slammed the door shut as soon as they were out.

CHAPTER 60

THE VORTEX HAD caught him once again. Vicks didn't have any place to go. He reached the Lodhi gardens and sat on the grass. Without a doubt, he would become the scapegoat. Not just the police, this time, but the intelligence and internal security guys were also on his back. It was frustrating. All he was trying to do was get his job back. But everything he'd done so far had backfired. He wondered if he could call ACP Rao. But this case was now well beyond the ACP. In fact, it was well beyond everyone.

In the end, he called his only insurance, ACP Rao, who picked up after two rings.

'I'm in trouble.'

'I know. Why didn't you tell me everything in Bangkok?'

Vicks had no reply.

'Where are you?'

'Lodhi garden.'

'I will be there in fifteen minutes.' The call was disconnected.

Vicks stared at the dead phone for a long time and finally, when he looked around absentmindedly, began to watch the mynahs and pigeons jumping about in the grass, searching for worms. The majestic stone tombs of former Muslim rulers stood around them. The walking path of the garden was filled with morning walkers moving up and down purposefully, their faces confident in taking on another day.

Though Vicks trusted ACP Rao, he knew the police could easily track him here. He switched his mobile phone off and summoned a young peanut seller.

'Want to earn a hundred rupees this morning?'

The boy, about fifteen, nodded greedily.

Vicks pulled a piece of paper out of his wallet, scribbled *American café, Habitat Center* on it, and gave it to the boy with a hundred-rupee note.

'If a policeman comes looking for me, give him this slip.' He described ACP Sachin Rao in detail. 'But remember, no one else.'

The boy smiled, grabbed the money and piece of paper, and walked away. Vicks was not sure if this was the best solution, but he knew that ACP Rao, upon not finding him, would certainly ask around.

He took an auto-rickshaw to the Habitat Center, arriving ten minutes later. The café had just opened, and he entered to the smell of eggs, coffee, and waffles.

After ordering coffee, he settled at the far end where he could clearly see the entrance. He didn't have to wait more than twenty minutes before the ACP sauntered inside and slipped onto the bench across from him.

He smiled in greeting, to which Vicks didn't respond, but he did offer his hand. The ACP settled for coffee too, which Vicks had consumed two cups of by now, but he asked for another one.

'There is only one way out of this—'

Vicks raised his hand to make him stop. 'Leave my dad out of this. I will never ask for a favour from him, even if I'll die without it.'

The ACP pushed his weight against the backrest, looked around as if he was trying to make up his mind about how to respond to this extreme reaction, and finally said, 'I was going to, but I won't.'

Vicks offered a weak smile. They sipped their coffee, and after about five minutes, Vicks asked, 'How long can I dodge the police and the others?'

'Two days if you are smart, which I have seen firsthand that you are, but only one day if you're unlucky. Remember, when it comes to passing verdict, in the eyes of the law, there is a difference between giving yourself up and being apprehended.'

'Noted.'

As if on an afterthought, Vicks told him about his escape from the room at the Mandarin Oriental hotel in Bangkok. He also shared Tonya's assessment about his getaway. ACP Rao's eyes narrowed as he heard the whole story, and when Vicks was done, the ACP had a hint of a smile on his face.

'I think your girlfriend is right. The killer let you go on purpose. But why would he do that?' The ACP banged on the table, and a few people around them were distracted from their conversations for a few seconds before they got caught up again and ignored them. 'Okay, let me think more about this, Vicks.'

They shook hands and departed within five minutes of one another.

CHAPTER 61

THE MEN AND women were brought into the building from five different locations. They arrived in trucks, tired after the long journey, their hands tied behind their backs. A chain kept them together, and as they moved into the building, soldiers in black overalls kicked them to make them move faster. The trucks arrived within half an hour of one another. By noon, with the men and women assembled in the central area of the building, the massive gates were closed and the chain joining the prisoners removed.

It was dark inside, and the prisoners had no idea what to expect next. After a few minutes, a bright overhead halogen lamp was switched on at one end. It patchily illuminated the building. Another was switched on at the other end, and slowly, as the lamps heated, there was sufficient light.

A voice reached them from the public address system. It was soft, like at a holy place, but what it said was devastating.

'You have been gathered here because you are our enemy. But we Iranians don't want to punish you. You will be punished by your own forces. Your airplanes, very soon, maybe in a few hours, will strike this building with missiles, thinking this place is storing chemical weapons. When they have blasted this place, we will tell them the contents of our package. You infidels, who have been caught spying in our territory, will be punished by your own country.'

The silence returned, and the hundred men and women stayed quiet. They'd known all along that they would die, but this kind of death added to the burden of their failure. Among them were spies who had traveled to Iran during the past ten years as journalists, doctors, or simply tourists. There were a few who were not spies but had simply been unlucky that they'd chosen to travel to Iran out of curiosity and been suspected by the Iranians.

People condemned to death don't like to speak, so there was no murmuring, no eye contact with each other, just blank eyes in expressionless faces. A few sat on the floor. No one was crying. There was nothing to repent; all the crying and frustration had been released already in captivity. Now they waited for the strike.

There was one man of about eighteen among them, a man who'd been captured just a few days ago and wasn't yet fully convinced his captors could be so cruel. He got up and walked to the closed iron gates. Once he reached them, he knocked, politely at first and then rather loudly, to make sure the people on the other side heard him.

None of the other prisoners reacted as he began to bang on the door, shouting, 'I know you won't kill us. Just open the door. Do a thorough investigation. I'm not a spy and I'm not going to die here.'

From somewhere above them, perhaps on the other side of the lights, a sharp sound cracked out and the young man slumped to the floor. He was dead in a second, his back a big hollow, eaten by the large bullet, and his face still caught in anticipation of a frank response.

Everyone ignored him.

The lights were dimmed and the voice spoke again. 'We don't want to kill you. Be happy that you are dying at the hands of your own people, using up your own arsenal.'

And then it was silent, like death itself.

CHAPTER 62

VICKS HAD BARELY left the American café in the Habitat Centre and started walking towards the exit when he saw ACP Rao again, his expression anxious.

'Vicks, we've tracked Jamie down. Of all the places in the world, he just landed in Kolkata from Bangkok on yet another British passport. The Thai police recognized him and alerted us.'

'So?'

'I have spoken to the police commissioner and gotten a special immunity for you. As long as you are with me, you won't be arrested. Let's do this together, Vicks, find the killer and arrest him. I will get my murderer, and you will no longer be a suspect in the killing. It is a win-win for both of us, what do you say?'

Vicks nodded and stepped aside to call Tonya. After a few minutes, he rejoined the ACP and nodded.

'Great! Let's head to the airport straightaway. We don't have a moment to lose.'

They walked to the ACP's jeep in the underground parking lot and were soon zipping along the roads of New Delhi on an exceptionally bright and sunny winter day. Vicks sat by the window, his nerves brittle and gaze empty. There was nowhere for him to go, and being under police protection was his best bet. Certainly safer than being with his boss, or in the protection of his own father.

In any case, by aligning himself with the police, he'd ensured that he was no longer a worm on the hook, but a part of the operational team that held the fishing rod.

When the two of them landed in Kolkata, a man was waiting for them who introduced himself as Biplab. His voice was oily and his face had pockmarks from some old disease. He looked about seventy, but it was perhaps the fatigue of being a policeman in Kolkata that had played on his personality and aged him. It was impossible to guess how old he really was; he could have been anything between fifty and sixty.

However, his eyes were sharp and purposeful. 'The suspect is heading north in a taxi towards Siliguri, maybe even Sikkim. We are following him using different vehicles in a relay.'

ACP Rao nodded.

'I have booked you two on a flight to Bagdogra. Luckily, it leaves in one hour. You will get your weapons there.'

ACP Rao's next nod sent him away. But not before Biplab had handed him an envelope containing their airline tickets.

Once they had settled inside the aircraft destined for Bagdogra, Vicks whispered, 'Do you think this is the best thing to do? We should be more worried about the attack on Israel, don't you think?'

'Thanks to your boss, everyone in the world who can stop that from happening knows about it. The authorities everywhere are working on it as we speak. Our job remains to nab a killer who has committed homicide on our soil.'

'Right.'

Vicks saw the logic and decided to nap a little. By the time the plane landed, it would be dark, and he had no idea what to expect during the night. Certainly not a comfortable nap.

CHAPTER 63

ARIEL HAD TRIED his best to locate Jamie in Bangkok. The Thai police did try to help, but without any success. In the process, he lost track of the journalist, Vicks. Finally, on arrival at the Delhi airport after his return from Bangkok, when he was calling his boss from the coffee shop just before exiting the airport, he saw Vicks, accompanied by another man, entering the domestic terminal after checking in. As soon as they were out of sight, he ambled across to the counter and learned that the two of them were on their way to Kolkata. Why Kolkata? he wondered.

Ariel called his boss again briefly with this revised information, bought a ticket using his phone, and checked in too. On the plane, he lifted his small bag to cover his face as he passed the spot where Vicks was seated and quickly walked to his seat, which was several rows behind him. He didn't want to be recognised. Vicks had run into him in the corridor of the Mandarin Oriental hotel in Bangkok when he'd been successful in escaping from Jamie's clutches, and then he'd seen him through the closing lift doors.

His boss had updated him about the articles published in the Indian media, and Ariel got a chance to read the disastrous news in the *India Now* newspaper on the plane, as he found the latest edition in the pocket on the back of the seat in front of him. It was a shock that the information contained in the piece of paper he had brought from Iran, for which a daughter of Israel had lost her life, was now common knowledge. This meant that the enemy would certainly try to change their plans, maybe move the entire factory overnight, or worse, attack the Israeli ships while they were still preparing for the strike.

The secret was no longer a secret. His anger towards Vicks rose, and it was only with great difficulty that he controlled himself. Why would they print such a story in the newspaper? How irresponsible of the Indian media.

By now, the aircraft had taken off and leveled off on an even course. The food service trolley arrived next to him. After he had accepted his food tray, the air hostess smiled and handed over a folded piece of paper. He looked at her, puzzled.

'Sir, this note has been sent by your friend, seated over there.' She pointed toward where Vicks was seated.

Ariel's cover was blown. He felt naked and vulnerable. The piece of paper only had a smiley face drawn on it. He folded it back up, slipped it into his shirt pocket, and closed his eyes.

This wasn't a good sign. It was perhaps time to collaborate with the Indians. He decided to call his boss once more when he landed in Kolkata.

CHAPTER 64

JAMIE WAS DRUNK. He was singing in the car and hadn't told the taxi driver his destination yet. His boss had summoned him to Sikkim when he told him about being followed in Bangkok.

'Bangkok is no longer safe, Jalaluddin. Head out as quickly as you can on an unused passport. Go to Kolkata and then on to Sikkim. Wait there for a few days. Then you can come back to London and stay here on paid holiday for a couple of months before we send you on your next assignment.'

It suited him fine. Ever since he'd fooled the long-nosed man who followed him down Khaosan Road in Bangkok, he'd been having the trip of his lifetime. Every prostitute who pleasured him, he called Sherry. Life was good fun, and he was looking forward to some special moments in Sikkim too.

'Where now, sir?' the driver turned his head to ask. 'We have reached Siliguri.'

'I'll get out here.'

He paid up and waited for the car to drive away, and then he hired another taxi and ordered him to drive to Sikkim before unscrewing the cap on another bottle of whiskey, which he'd bought at the airport.

Night was approaching, but there was sufficient light to see the Teesta River in the gorge below. One side of the mountains had a golden glow, their jagged tops lit by the last of the light, while on the other side, the mountains were soaked in darkness. The sight was magical, and he reclined on the seat, his legs extended under the driver's seat to the fullest extent they could. He wondered what Sherry would have said had she been with him at this moment. He imagined her, a smile playing on his lips, and had a pretend conversation with her.

'Sherry, this is beautiful, isn't it?'

He spoke on her behalf: 'Yes, it is, and I love you.'

The conversation went on as he drank more and more. In another half an hour, feeling drowsy, he slipped into a deep sleep. When the driver shook him sometime later, he realised that they had stopped.

'Where now?'

Jamie told him the address, thinking what the hell, there wouldn't be anyone looking for him in a forgotten place like this. The air was cooler, and he stuck his head out the window to feel the cold.

When they arrived at a bungalow in the far corner of the city, Jamie stepped out and stretched his hands over his head. Across the way, lights were twinkling in the faraway villages in the valley, and the road ended where he stood. It was a perfect place to stay hidden while enjoying worldly pleasures. How thoughtful. He had asked his boss for a supply of alcohol and women. His boss had laughed and said, almost like a don to his son in a Hollywood movie, 'You got it. Take a week off and hit as many as you like.'

Jamie waited for the glow of the taxi's taillights to fade away and then walked up to the house. The bungalow lay in darkness, and he didn't have the keys. He knocked and waited.

A man opened the door, coughed, and asked him to come in. Jamie was hoping a pretty woman would open it, but he could understand the need to have a caretaker. He followed the man into a candlelit living room, where another man was seated.

'Sit down.' The sitting man had steel in his voice. This wasn't a caretaker's voice. This man was in the business of doing dirty things. Jamie's brain kicked to life. He casually looked around, needing to assess the situation before he could take any action. He didn't have a gun, as he was coming straight from the airport, and he missed having a weapon.

The living room smelt of disuse and was ripe with dampness. Was he at the wrong house? Or worse, had the adversary somehow got wind of his trip and taken over the property?

He obeyed, but as he tried to sit, he lost balance and fell on the floor. The other man, the one who had opened the door and was now standing behind him, had kicked the chair away. The two of them laughed.

'Can't you see where the chair is? Or you are too drunk, Mr. Jalaluddin?'

So they even knew his real name. Who were these men? He got to his feet and waited for the situation to unfold, weaponless and confused.

The man in front of him picked up a knife from a table that Jamie hadn't noticed before. The blade reflected the candlelight as the man moved closer to him. He stopped five feet away. The man behind him gave him a glass of water to drink. Now he knew what it meant. He didn't fight it and drank the drugged liquid. He was now aware what was in store, but he clung to hope, to the impossible.

The two men waited, and when he was completely immobilized, the one with the knife moved forward and placed the cold blade on his neck. The time had come. He was going to die, and he wanted them to ask what his last wish was. He deserved that much after all he'd done for Islam. *If they did ask, what would my last wish be?* he wondered. *Meet Sherry after death or be given a generous supply of whiskey? Either of them? Both? But which one, if I could have only one?*

'You Christian pig,' the man with the knife shouted while Jamie contemplated his choices. As his throat was cut, he knew the answer. It was whiskey.

The men left him in the damp room and walked away. A kilometer from the bungalow, they picked up their motorcycle and rode off into the night. Their faces were flushed, like after sex. They had killed one more infidel.

Chapter 65

Vicks and ACP Rao arrived at the Bagdogra airport and waited for the police to update them on the location of their quarry. By then, it was dark, and the next call from Biplab revealed their destination.

'The target changed taxis, but he was so drunk that he had no idea he was being followed. He arrived in Sikkim a few minutes ago. Here's the address.'

ACP Rao noted the address. 'Don't refuse to give your professional team credit, Biplab, just because the target was drunk.'

Biplab grunted over the phone, said he agreed, and disconnected. Night driving in the hilly terrain could be a tricky affair, so they chose a taxi driver who seemed experienced enough and left the airport within minutes.

The drive would take three hours, mused Vicks. It meant they would arrive at their destination at midnight, which was a good time, as their target might be fast asleep, exhausted by travel, alcohol, and probably some other corporeal pleasures.

'Tell me about yourself, ACP Rao, sir.'

They were really too tired to talk, but to keep themselves from falling asleep, they chatted for a while, and when a *dhaba* floated into view at about ten, they ordered the taxi to stop. Their last meal before going into action was simple and light. They didn't touch alcohol. Their journey resumed after fifteen minutes.

Vicks asked for the car to be stopped about a kilometer short of the address, and keeping to the shadows, the two of them traveled the rest of the way on foot. Upon arriving, they realized it was a bungalow enveloped in darkness.

ACP Rao had declined the help of the local police, as this was a special operation, but he now wondered if that was the right thing to do. Without backup, night-vision devices, proper weapons, or any means of communication between the two of them if they used different points to gain entry, the odds were stacked against them. Perhaps it was a better idea to wait until morning, as nothing was likely to happen during the night. Having reached his *bolthole*, the target would definitely stay put there.

'Do you think we should wait until morning?' he whispered to Vicks.

'I think we should. It's too risky now. The enemy knows the layout of the house; we don't.'

The ACP smiled, then realized Vicks would not to be able to see him in the darkness and pressed his forearm to convey his agreement. Within minutes, they found a bush off to one side, near where the road ended. It was a perfect hiding place, as from there, they could see the entrance of the bungalow clearly. The ACP pulled out the 9 mm pistol that had been given to him by a policeman on the instructions of Biplab when he arrived at Bagdogra airport and settled in to wait, Vicks by his side.

CHAPTER 66

SHERRY'S FATHER RAISED himself from the mat. Prayers were over. Though he was free now, and on his way to India, he still read the Koran. Reading the Koran had become a habit, formed while pretending to be a Muslim all those years in Tehran. He couldn't just kick the habit now. So he decided to continue, and continued going by his Muslim name as well.

The ten by ten room was on the second floor of the house. It contained one small cot, a mat for prayers, a steel jug on a small table next to the bed, and a poster of Mecca in an elaborate gold frame on one of the walls.

A young boy of about ten peeped into the small room where he sat, pulling the curtain to one side. The old man was a guest of the boy's family, which lived in the three rooms on the ground floor, but he did not know the boy's family or their names. He had just knocked on their door the previous night and, after the greetings were over, asked if he could stay for a few hours. The couple had smiled and given him a room and fed him too. Twice. He was grateful.

In a few minutes, the old man was prepared to leave, but the boy held his hand and kept him from going. He looked into the boy's eyes and smiled. The boy let him go after his father urged him to. The couple bid him farewell and didn't even ask him for money, which in any case, he had very little of. What he had, he wanted to hold onto for as long as possible.

After hitchhiking for another day, he reached the border city of Sialkot in Pakistan. He was still grieving his daughter's death, but freedom had diluted his sadness. He looked at the open sky for hours now and smiled when the sun rose or set. He smiled at the birds chirping, water gushing, and dogs chasing rabbits in the open fields. His daughter was dead, and he couldn't change that. But he was free. Still, what was she doing in Delhi, in a cheap hotel, and who had killed her?

The purpose of his journey was twofold. One, to visit the room where his daughter had breathed her last and bid her a final farewell, and two, to warn his country of the wicked designs of the enemy. He had in reality become a practicing Muslim, not out of choice but habit, and had stopped believing in the human-made barriers of boundaries and religion, yet his overall aim of saving lives remained.

The tricky part would be crossing the border into Jammu and Kashmir, which he was hoping to do in the early hours before dawn, when the guards would be least attentive. He would swim across the Tawi River, which ran next to the Bajwat Wildlife Sanctuary. The old man had been on the road now for four days but had taken care to eat well. In his youth, he had been a good swimmer and was therefore confident of reaching the other side without much difficulty.

He left just after dinner. Keeping a few feet away from the road, he passed the Sialkot cantonment and continued toward the sanctuary. Along the way, he stopped for a while to let his muscles relax before continuing further. The timing of his crossing was important, and he knew he would have to use up every reserve of energy in his body to be well inside Indian Territory before sunrise.

By three in the morning, he reached a spot from which he could see the river. Wolves howling from the sanctuary to his left welcomed his arrival, and he smiled at the absurdity. There was a watch tower not far from where he stood, and he wondered if there were dogs on the prowl under it. He entered the river and walked about a kilometer downstream to shake off any possible trail if sniffer dogs did indeed appear out of nowhere. Once he was sure he'd put a reasonable distance between his last position and his new one, he reclined under a tree and began taking deep breaths.

The moon was in its first quarter, so it was impossible for him to see the other side. He had no idea how wide the river was or where it was the narrowest. Finally, at about four in the morning, he looked eastwards, said a brief prayer, and jumped into the water. The newspaper clipping, his only possession, was carefully wrapped in layers of polyethene in the pocket of his loose trousers.

It took him an hour to reach the other side. He was completely exhausted and shivered uncontrollably. It was at that moment that he heard the barking of dogs. He looked back at the river and knew there was no way he could go back. He had underestimated the Indians watching the border. He saw a flashlight moving up and down and heard a pack of sniffer dogs heading his way. The old man had perhaps five minutes to decide his next course of action. He closed his eyes and waited.

CHAPTER 67

THERE WAS A man approaching. The time was about two in the morning, and Vicks' muscles tightened. This meant trouble, an unexpected crisis. The man seemed familiar, and he was walking directly towards them without much caution.

ACP Rao slipped the safety on his pistol to the firing position. The air began to thicken around them. Vicks swallowed, not sure if his nervousness was audible.

They waited until the man stopped about five feet from them. He peered into the darkness and whispered, 'I'm just an Israeli friend trailing you from Delhi. You know me, don't you?'

Vicks had seen him on the airplane, but when they departed from Kolkata, he'd been sure that they'd lost him. But they obviously hadn't, and now he was here, adding a new dimension to their predicament.

'If we work together as a team, we can do wonders. You know what's at stake, Mr. Vicks. You're all over the news.' His tone wasn't friendly.

It was natural for him to behave like this, under the circumstances, Vicks thought. But Vicks had been working alone from the start, and it was the police who had made him a collaborator. They weren't exactly a team, though they might have looked like one at the moment. Vicks' sole intention was to play whatever role was necessary to see that Jamie was arrested, leaving him in the clear.

Vicks elbowed ACP Rao.

'Okay, remove your gun and place it on the ground,' ACP Rao controlled his voice well.

'I am not carrying a weapon.'

Vicks stepped closer and frisked him thoroughly. He was indeed not carrying a gun.

After ACP Rao introduced himself to Ariel, smiling the whole time because the man had no clue that the ACP knew who he was, a five-minute discussion established the fact that they were on the same side. And that the killer holed up in the bungalow opposite them had murdered an Israeli citizen in cold blood. Their job was limited, at that moment, to apprehend the criminal and, if he resisted, using any force necessary.

'Okay, here's the plan,' began ACP Rao. 'At daybreak, Mr. Ariel will approach from the rear as Vicks knocks on the front door to get their attention.' They'd agreed that they could not afford to assume Jamie was alone in there and decided to plan accordingly. 'That will shift their focus to the front. Hopefully. I will cover the door with my pistol from the hedge in the front lawn. Okay?'

If he disagreed with the plan, the Israeli didn't show it. After a few moments, he said he was fine with it.

Just after dawn, as soon as there was sufficient light to see, Vicks walked across to the wrought iron gates. He kept his hands hanging loosely at his sides and his gait normal, as directed by ACP Rao. The Israeli had taken his position behind the house and would be starting at the same time. They had synchronized their watches. The gate had a latch that opened without much effort.

Vicks walked towards the door, his heart beating wildly. Was this really necessary? After all, he wasn't the police. Why couldn't the ACP do this with Vicks watching from outside with the gun? He ignored the fact that he wasn't trained to fire a pistol from nearly a hundred feet. He thought about Tonya, aware that criminals were watching him from inside the house.

When Vicks reached the door, he paused for a few seconds to catch his breath before knocking. They had practiced the first few sentences that Vicks would speak.

No one answered the door. Vicks looked over his shoulder but couldn't spot the ACP, then knocked again. He tried a third time after a few seconds, and this time, he heard feet shuffling inside. This was the moment. He hoped they didn't spot the lie in his first sentence. And if they did, that the ACP was able to do something with his gun quickly to scatter them, giving Vicks the opportunity and cover to escape.

The door opened and before Vicks could speak, his eyes widened. Ariel stood in front of him.

'Welcome to the house of death, Mr. Vicks.' With this, he turned and walked back down the dark corridor. Vicks froze in position, but when he heard the Israeli call from somewhere inside, he walked in with hesitant steps. When he arrived in the living room, he saw the body of a dead man sitting in a chair.

He crossed to the other side of the room and saw Jamie looking out the window. The curtains had been opened on one side, and the morning light fell on his face. Just like the woman he had killed a few days before, he looked like someone caught in a momentary daze. Except his neck had been cut deeply and blood had spilled all over him.

'There's no one else here,' Ariel said and sat down on a sofa chair. They heard someone coming in and turned in alarm but relaxed when they saw ACP Rao charge in, his pistol appearing before he did. But the scene inside the room erased his caution.

'I think we need to call the local cops now,' declared ACP Rao. He raised his cell phone to his ear.

Half an hour later, a police siren broke the silence in the room where the three of them sat and waited. As the ACP began the process of handing over the scene of the crime to the local police team, Ariel and Vicks stepped outside onto the lawn.

'You were lucky in Bangkok, Mr. Vicks,' Ariel said as they stopped in the middle of the lawn.

'Yeah.'

'Tell me: why did you write that story for the newspaper? That's so unprofessional, don't you think?' Ariel was looking straight into his eyes.

'The obvious is sometimes not that obvious, Mr. Ariel.'

'You mean the story is wrong?'

He shifted his weight from one foot to the other. 'I didn't say that. I just pointed out that you are assuming I wrote that story.'

'Your name is there... clearly you can't blame someone else for it.'

Vicks thought for a second. If there was someone to be blamed for it, it was his boss. He felt let down and cheated. Though it was unethical to share an editor-reporter conversation with a foreign spy, Vicks still went ahead and explained the whole situation to him.

The ACP joined them after ten minutes.

'So, Vicks, you are now in the clear for Sherry Bing's murder. We hope to find the murderer's DNA in the Paharganj hotel to connect him to the crime. We will also use the statement of that ramshackle tea stall owner you told me about. I have told the Delhi police to locate him and get him to the mortuary by the time the dead man's body reaches there later today.'

CHAPTER 68

THE OLD MAN straightened up. He had to find his daughter's killers, and he also had to warn his country against striking Iran's positions. The man who had slipped the newspaper clipping under his cell door and later planned his escape had shared with him that Israel had been provided with false information about Iran possessing chemical weapons, and if they bombed the indicated positions, many people would perish without reason.

He mustered every last bit of energy in his body and ran into Indian Territory at an angle away from where he could hear the dogs. Luckily, he was soon in a field with a standing mustard crop that gobbled him up hungrily. He ran like never before. After about an hour, he was out of breath to such a degree that his legs buckled under him and he fell. It was cold, and there was a lot of early morning dew, which was likely to work in his favour, as it would throw the dogs off his track. After a few moments, he got up and began to run again, slower this time, hoping it would help him to run for a longer time.

He couldn't believe it, but he was successful in not getting caught. He arrived at the periphery of a village and was attracted by the smoke emanating from the houses. He wanted tea and some warm clothing.

But that was too big a risk to take. He continued until about midday. By that point, he had put about a dozen villages between the border patrol and himself. He was, at last, safe.

'Train to Delhi?' he asked a tea stall seller in English. With no Indian currency, he knew he couldn't buy anything. The Pakistani rupees and U.S. dollars that he was given by his benefactor back in the jail were of no use.

The young man pointed out the right direction.

The old man nodded and asked, 'I don't have money, free chai?'

The young man looked at him and his expression changed. As the old man was about to turn and walk away, he smiled and said, 'Okay.'

The old man savoured the tea, his eyes constantly on the glass jar in which biscuits were kept.

The young man must have observed it. 'Take one,' he said. The old man hesitated, and the tea seller persisted, 'No problem. Afghani?'

The old man was taken aback by the question. Then he realized how his fair complexion, beard, and manner of his dress must look. He walked away without answering.

The town he had reached was Ranbir Singh Pura. Out on the road, he was lucky enough to get a lift in a truck and arrived in Jammu that night. In Jammu, he exchanged his U.S. dollars and rented a small hotel room, just to freshen up. He changed into new clothes that he bought—a shirt, trousers, and jacket—and trimmed his beard again, and was soon on his way to the railway station.

He bought a non-reserved ticket to Delhi and hopped on the first passenger train that was pulling in that direction. But now that he was cleaned up, he was very clearly a foreigner, a white man who stood out among his fellow passengers, who were all different shades of brown. This was a real problem. He had no passport and no way to prove his identity. If he was arrested, his mission would remain unfinished and hundreds would die in the attack on the factory in Tehran.

At the next station, therefore, he got off, waited for a goods train, and quietly slipped aboard a car that was carrying sand. The car was open, with no roof, and the night was really cold, but with the food he had eaten in Jammu in his stomach, he was ready to brave it.

CHAPTER 69

'IN DELHI AIRPORT, they shook hands—Vicks, ACP Rao, and Ariel—and went their separate ways. ACP Rao had assured Vicks that he would ensure that the Delhi police didn't bother him, but said that Vicks should not leave Delhi without informing him.

It was late afternoon when Vicks boarded the airport metro. Upon his arrival back in Delhi, his thoughts had again turned to money. All the expenses of the Kolkata trip had been paid for by ACP Rao, but now Vicks was back to paying for himself. A taxi would have cost a lot and made him reach his destination early. He wanted to be home by six, in time to surprise Tonya. In the end, he made it at about half past five. He let himself into her flat using the spare key and inhaled her smell deeply.

After a quick wash, he prepared some coffee and sat down by the window to wait. He heard noises outside even before he could take his first sip. He opened the door, and Tonya's mouth rounded in surprise. Before she could do anything, he hugged her, lifting her off her feet. After a few breathless kisses, he offered her the coffee.

'Good, now no more of that story,' Tonya concluded, even before he could fill her in on all the details. He had sent the story about the finding of

Sherry's killer in Sikkim to a rival newspaper. When they asked how much money he wanted for it, he had said nothing and just hung up. His boss from *India Now* had called later, after he must have seen the article online, but Vicks didn't take his call. He needed money, but a man had to have ethics.

'It's over, Tonya. The murderer has been found. He was killed by someone before we got there. For the first time, I didn't feel sad seeing a dead man.'

Tonya stayed quiet, sipping her coffee. Night slowly enveloped their house and the room got darker.

Tonya had just gotten up to switch the lights on when the phone rang. It was Raju Arora.

'Vicks, I have information for you.' His voice was barely audible.

'What is it?'

'There is a man in that dead woman's room. He came here and asked for that specific room. I thought he was a tourist, but when I took him into the room, he sat down on the sofa and began to cry.'

'Who is he?'

'I'm not sure, but the way he is crying, he must be the father of the girl. I just don't know what to do.'

'Where is he now?'

'In the room. Our hotel only reopened today, and now this. I don't know what to do. Shall I call the police?'

'No, listen carefully. Wait for him to calm down, and when he does, please tell him not to leave the room. I have to interview him. Just tell him you've called someone who knows who the killer is. I will be there in fifteen minutes tops.'

Vicks left that very second. He took an auto-rickshaw to Paharganj and, when they arrived, paid the driver a hundred rupees and left without waiting for his change. There was no one at the reception desk when he barged into the Le Yogi Deluxe Hotel, so he climbed the stairs two at a time. He knew where Sherry was killed and was soon at the door. It was ajar, and he pushed it open.

A man sat on the sofa next to the empty bed, his head hanging, his hands shaking slightly, and his back curved. Raju stood to one side, his back against the wall, face expressionless. Vicks closed the door, walked across the room, and stopped two feet from the man.

When the man lifted his head, Vicks realized just how old he was. And frail, almost lifeless. His eyes were red, and he had an aimless air about him, like someone who had lost it all.

'I am sorry. Are you Sherry's father?'

Vicks knew that this was the one time the man shouldn't have to answer any questions, but he had no choice. Grief was best handled with objectivity, his experience had taught him.

The old man locked eyes with him for what seemed like over a minute. Then he took a long breath and spoke, 'Yes.'

Vicks waited for more, but the old man went back to his stooped posture, as if to indicate that the

conversation was over and now he should be left alone
with his grief.

'Your daughter's killer has been found.'

Vicks expected an extreme reaction, and that was
exactly what he got. The old man jumped to his feet,
his hands grabbed Vicks' collar, and he shook him hard.
But no words came out. The emotion had choked his
voice, his thinking, his ability to organise his thoughts.
The old man released him just as suddenly and flopped
back into the sofa chair.

'The killer is dead too. We don't know who killed
him, but he is dead as a doornail.'

The old man didn't respond, but Vicks noticed that
a muscle that had been twitching on his jaw stopped.
He also relaxed visibly, like a dry cloth on a clothing
hook when it gets drenched in a sudden rain.

'Who are you?' The old man seemed to be getting in
control of the situation. Vicks told him everything. All
the facts, including the story of the chemical weapons
in Tehran, which had been wrongly attributed to him
in the article.

'That is a lie,' murmured the old man.

'What? How do you know?' Vicks was taken
aback, his mind juggling the possible reasons.

The old man told Vicks about himself, and
that made it clearer for Vicks. He started slowly,
deliberately, and by the time he finished with all the
details about why he was here, both Vicks and Raju
were staring at him with their mouths open. 'You seem

like a good person, my son. Please use this information to stop this madness.'

'Thank you, Mr. Bing.'

'Can I leave for the embassy?'

'Sure. But just a minute. I have something for you.' Vicks flipped his phone open and showed him the picture of Sherry that he had taken after he arrived in the hotel the morning she was killed. She looked alive, her eyes open and skin glowing. The old man took the phone from Vick's hand and cried some more.

'My daughter said once, "Dad, if I leave this world before you, my last thoughts will be about you." This picture is precious to me. I know she is thinking about me.'

Vicks offered to email it to the old man, but he said he didn't have an email address. Vicks said he would figure out a way to get it to him. Then he pulled out the bus ticket for the last journey of his unfortunate daughter. The old man rolled it in his fingers like it was a precious metal and placed it in his pocket.

'Shalom!' And he was gone.

CHAPTER 70

'THANK YOU, RAJU.' The room seemed so empty after the old man left that Vicks almost thought his own voice echoed.

'I'm sorry about letting you down, Vicks. It won't happen again.' Raju's voice was replete with sincerity, and Vicks thought of the many times they'd had good fun together.

'Sure, it's cool.'

Raju stepped forward and hugged Vicks. When he stepped away, Vicks noticed he was crying.

There was no time to lose. Vicks was able to put two and two together now. In Bangkok, he'd been used as a messenger, someone who was baited with information and sent away, his escape deliberately planned. And now that Sherry's father had told him the truth, he knew that the information published by *India Now* was false. Perhaps, he thought, he could swing the whole thing his way and maybe gain from it.

Vicks rushed to the rival newspaper's office. There, he filed a new story, stating that there were *no* chemical weapons in Tehran and that the story published by *India Now* was an exaggeration in which he was deliberately misquoted.

By the time he returned home, it was midnight, but Tonya was waiting for him. They were chatting after a special dinner that she had cooked for him when the phone rang. It was the editor at the rival newspaper. Vicks listened to him, his smile widening, and when he finally disconnected, he hugged Tonya. They had offered him a job as a reporter at a salary thirty percent higher than what he'd been paid at *India Now* at the time he was fired.

No words were required. They made love, and afterwards, slept in each other's arms without a care in the world.

The next morning, after Tonya had left for the hospital, Vicks called Ariel. They met at a café half an hour later.

'Hello!' Vicks shook his hand. He ordered Assam tea, while Ariel settled for a latte.

'How close were you to firing missiles at that building near Tehran when you got the right intel?' asked Vicks as he added more sugar to his tea.

'Minutes.'

'What happens next?'

'An ugly man disappears.'

'I could find you among millions because of your nose, Mr. Ariel.'

Ariel laughed and sized himself up in his reflection in the window.

They drank their beverages in silence, and when done, each paid for himself and left, smiling equally widely.

EPILOGUE

A YEAR HAS passed.

Vicks and Tonya are still together. There have been minor issues, but overall, they are doing just fine. Vicks received a thirty-percent raise after The Association of Print & Electronic Media named him 'The Best Investigative Reporter of 2017'. There was a cash prize of one lakh rupees, and Vicks bought a car using the money and a loan from the car dealer. It's a blue hatchback that Tonya likes very much because it matches the sofa in their drawing room. Vicks has stopped drinking rum, though he misses it sometimes. Once, he bought a bottle on the way home from the office, opened it in the new car, and was about to gulp, but stopped. Somehow, it didn't feel right. There was a dustbin nearby, and he lobbed it in. The bottle hit the rim of the plastic container, did a little dance, and disappeared into it. Vicks does like to sometimes drink wine or beer with Tonya; that's the green zone. He has been contemplating proposing to Tonya for a few weeks now. Hopefully soon. He loves her a lot.

Vicks' father has been transferred to Mumbai, and Vicks is happy with this development. His father calls him sometimes, and Vicks ignores his calls. Once, in a dream, he saw his father shouting at him and woke up in alarm. Just last week, his father sent him text saying that he was in the hospital and wanted him to visit. Vicks wanted to send a one-word reply: Sissy. He typed it out but deleted it before hitting the send button. Ultimately, he chose not to reply.

ACP Rao & his wife are expecting a baby in two months. He'd promised her once again that he would be home on their anniversary. It is today, but he is in Kolkata. Vicks and Tonya briefly visit her in the morning to present a bouquet. The ACP's wife is a lovely woman, a charming host but very quiet, perhaps due to the fact that her husband is not around. They eat the cake and leave.

Ariel has used his contacts to get the only woman in the world who's ever called him handsome out of Tehran. She lives with him in Vienna now, where he is on a new assignment.

The old man, Sherry Bing's father, passed away a month ago in Tel Aviv. He was cremated and interred next to his daughter. Her last picture and the bus ticket were cremated with him, as per his last wishes.

Alpha, Jamie's boss, has retired and is now on a world tour. At the moment, he is in London, staying in a posh hotel near Kensington gardens. He has made a new young friend there, one whose family is also staying in the same hotel. The seventeen-year old told him that his father's name is Arik Golan and he was an admiral in the Israeli Navy until recently. Alpha has met the boy's father only once and shook hands. 'It's a small world,' he had winked and got the same reply.

Harish, the receptionist, came from Udaipur with

his wife to visit Delhi a week ago. Vicks and Tonya met up with them and treated them to a nice dinner in Connaught place. The couple has invited them to visit them in Udaipur, which Vicks has accepted, though he has no such plans.

Jamie was cremated and interred in a Christian cemetery, as all the documents found on him were fake and showed him to be of that faith. His final resting place is in Sikkim, on the edge of town. His parents in London are hopeful that he will call them soon. His epitaph reads: Daniel Alphonso, 2017. There is no date of birth.